FIVE-YARD FULLER
of the N. Y. GNATS

Five-Yard Fuller was watching the hapless New York Gnats lose when he caught a foul ball. Because Ma Fuller had often said it "weren't right to keep anything which ain't yours," he walked over to the Gnat dugout to return the ball. Before he recovers from this and other surprises, Manager Big Noise Winnetka signs Fuller as pitcher for the tenth place Gnats. With the aid of some weird pitches, such as the Garter Snake Outshoot, Fuller and the Gnats climb out of the cellar and into the World Series. The rules of the game are never broken, but they are stretched to their outer limits.

FIVE-YARD FULLER
of the N.Y. GNATS

By Bob Wells

Illustrated by Harold Eldridge

G. P. Putnam's Sons   New York

To Maude Dennison Wells

FIVE-YARD FULLER
of the N. Y. GNATS

⊖ 1 ⊖

Bᴵᴳ Noise Winnetka, manager of the New York Gnats, hurried up the dugout steps to watch a fly ball sail lazily toward Four-Fingers Fibich in right field. A stranger would have supposed it was an easy out. But Winnetka and the St. Louis batter knew better. The batter went tearing around first and headed full tilt for second. The manager clasped his hands together prayerfully.

"Maybe this is the time," he said. "He hasn't caught one all year, but maybe this is the one. If he catches it we still might win this game."

Four-Fingers looked supremely confident. He jogged in a few steps, slapping his fist into the pocket of his glove. He jogged a few steps to the right. Then he reversed himself, ran full speed to the left, backed up a couple of steps, changed his mind, ran forward

7

and finally jumped high in the air with his glove outstretched. Big Noise groaned and covered his eyes
with his hand.

"What happened?" he asked the third-base coach,
Johnny Hobbes. "I can't bear to look."

Hobbes slapped him joyfully on the back.

"He caught it, that's what happened."

"He caught it? You're putting me on."

"It's true. First he ran too far to the right, then too
far to the left, then he jumped for it."

"I saw that much. But when he jumped it looked
like it was going to hit him on the head. That's when I
quit looking."

"It did hit him on the head. Then it bounced about
twenty feet straight up in the air and Four-Fingers fell
down. As he fell he rolled over on his back and put his
glove up to keep the sun out of his eyes and the ball
caught right in the webbing. That's the third out and
we're still tied going into the ninth."

The players came running off the field. Several of
them crowded around Fibich to congratulate him.

"That's using the old head, boy," Mule Bradshaw
told him. "And you've got the lump to prove it."

Fibich accepted the compliment modestly.

"Like I keep explaining to you guys," he said, "all it
takes to catch the ball is four fingers and a thumb. I
hope the rest of you was watching. Maybe you learned
something."

Big Noise raised his voice and started telling everyone within three hundred yards that it would be a
good idea for the Gnats to score some runs so they
could finally break their losing streak. But no one paid

much attention. He stopped talking when he felt a tug on his sleeve. He looked around. The most muscular young man he'd ever seen was holding out a scuffed baseball toward him.

"What're you doing on the playing field?" Winnetka demanded. "Spectators aren't allowed down here."

"I'm sorry, Mr. Big Noise," the young man said. "But I was sitting up there along the third-base line, watching the game, when the batter hit a foul right at me. I reached up and caught it. That was ten minutes ago. I'd of been here sooner only fifteen or twenty ushers tried to keep me from climbing over the railing."

The manager was getting impatient. It was bad enough to be in the midst of the longest losing streak in the history of baseball without having to deal with people like this.

"What is it you want, anyhow?"

"Why, like I told you, Mr. Big Noise, I caught this here baseball. It don't belong to me, so I'm bringing it back."

"You're what?"

"Returning it. Ma always told us Fullers never to keep nothing that don't belong to us."

Winnetka started to explain that it was customary for spectators to keep foul balls if they were lucky enough to catch them. Then he decided he had more important things to do. Skeeter Ferrara was leading off the inning and the count on him was already no balls and two strikes.

"Get out of here," the manager ordered. "Go back to your seat. Quit bothering me. Don't you realize if the Gnats lose this game it'll be thirty-four in a row?

We've already broken last year's record. The most we lost in a row last year was thirty-two."

"Sure, Mr. Big Noise. Only what'll I do with this baseball?"

"What do I care? Throw it to the batboy."

"That kid over there by the chicken wire?"

"You mean the screen. Yeah, that's the one. Throw it to him. Then get out of my hair."

Winnetka had his cap off, wiping his brow. The large young man considered pointing out that the manager didn't have any hair for him to get out of, but he decided it wouldn't be polite. He waved at the batboy, wound up and threw. The boy lunged for the ball. He missed it by a good three feet.

Winnetka reached up and grabbed the stranger's massive shoulder.

"Hey, what kind of a pitch was that?"

"Oh, that was nothing special, Mr. Big Noise. Back home in Rock Creek, I used to call that my garter-snake outshoot. It's sort of a triple curve. Well, now, I'm sorry to of bothered you and I'll just be getting on back up in the stands like you said."

The manager kept a firm grip on the shoulder. Skeeter Ferrara had struck out and Mule Bradshaw was at bat, but Winnetka ignored them. For the first time since the Gnats had hired him as manager there was a faint gleam of hope in his eyes. Johnny Hobbes came hurrying over.

"What's going on here? Who's this fellow? He doesn't belong down here on the field."

"You could say the same about most of our players," Winnetka reminded him. "I don't know who this kid is, but in thirty-seven years in baseball I never saw a pitch like the one he just threw."

Hobbes tilted his head back and peered up at the stranger. There was something familiar about the guileless blue eyes, the shock of straw-colored hair, the muscles. Especially the muscles.

"Five-Yard Fuller!" Hobbes shouted. "I saw you beat the Eagles in the playoff last fall." He turned to Winnetka. "You must have heard of this kid. He made the Knights champions of pro football practically singlehanded. He's the greatest back I've ever seen."

The manager shook his head. He said he never paid much attention to what was going on in other sports. He had troubles enough worrying about the Gnats and baseball.

"But never mind that. Grab a glove, Johnny. Let this kid toss a few to you. I want to see if that last pitch was a freak."

Hobbes took a catcher's mitt and walked over to the warmup area next to the stands. Mule Bradshaw had just popped out to the St. Louis shortstop and Four-Fingers Fibich was walking confidently toward home plate, swinging two bats. Winnetka handed Fuller a baseball and stood behind him, raising himself on tiptoe to peer over his shoulder.

"Go ahead. Throw another one like the one you threw at the batboy."

"The garter-snake outshoot? Okay, Mr. Big Noise."

Five-Yard wound up and threw. Hobbes, who had been an all-star catcher in his days as a player, leaned to the right, then to the left, then lunged right again, barely managing to grab the ball. He held it up and looked at it.

11

"I saw it, but I don't believe it."

Winnetka hurried over to him.

"What did it do, exactly?"

"Well, it started out as a curve to the right. Then it whipped around to the left. Finally, when it was almost to the plate, it curved right again."

Five-Yard had followed the manager. He stood there, grinning.

"That's why we used to call it the garter-snake outshoot, back at Rock Creek Consolidated," he said. "You ever watch a garter snake scooting through the grass when a gander's chasing him? That's just how he goes."

The crowd had set up a roar. The manager whirled on his heel to see what was happening. Four-Fingers Fibich had smashed the ball into the left-field bleachers. He was loping around the bases, doffing his batting helmet to the fans.

"Hey, we're ahead fourteen to thirteen going into the bottom of the ninth," Hobbes said. "Now if we only had a pitcher who could hold the Cards . . . Who've we got left, Big Noise?"

"I've already used seven pitchers in this game. That leaves Hoss Hill."

Hobbes groaned. It was true that Hoss seldom allowed a hit, but that was because he seldom got the ball near enough to the plate for the batters to swing at it. The last time he'd pitched he had walked six men straight before he'd been taken out. And that had been one of his better days. Hobbes turned back to the manager, shaking his head in despair. But a gleam of hope was still in Winnetka's eyes.

"Johnny, aren't we one under the player limit?"

"Yeah. Max Sparta quit this morning. He said he couldn't stand it the way his children looked at him when he had to tell them he played for the New York Gnats."

"And if we're one under the player limit, there's nothing to stop us from hiring a new man, is there?"

Hobbes began to feel a surge of hope himself. He looked at Five-Yard.

"Not a thing, Big Noise. I don't know if we've got a uniform big enough to fit him, but—"

"Well, fellows," Fuller said, "I guess I ought to go on back to my seat and see how the game comes out. I paid two and a half bucks for my seat and Ma always says you ought to get your money's worth."

He waved cordially at them and started to walk away. Hobbes grabbed one of his arms. Winnetka grabbed the other. The Gnats' catcher, Mike McBride, had just made the third out but neither the manager nor the coach was paying attention. They were too busy propelling Five-Yard down the dugout steps and into the dressing room, where Hobbes threw a uniform at him and Winnetka thrust a contract under his nose.

"But all I did was come over here to St. Louis to watch a ball game," Fuller protested. "I wasn't figuring on anything like this."

"Neither were we," Winnetka told him. "But there isn't time to argue about it. Just sign your name right there and you're a member of the worst team in the history of organized baseball."

"Well," Five-Yard said, picking up the pen, "I guess it wouldn't be polite to turn down an honor like that."

14

The bottom of the ninth had already begun. Hoss Hill had taken his warmup throws, getting every pitch right over home plate. The first St. Louis batter walked up. Mike McBride signaled for a fast ball on the outside corner. Hoss nodded solemnly, wound up and threw the ball into the stands. Mike signaled for a low curve. It hit the ground three feet in front of home plate. McBride ripped off his mask and started toward the mound. But then he stopped. He shrugged. He knew that nothing he could say would help. He went back and crouched behind home plate and concentrated on trying to catch the ball. From long experience, he knew that with Hoss Hill pitching it might go anywhere between first base and third. Anywhere, that is, but over the plate.

Johnny Hobbes came running up the dugout steps and called time out. He walked as slowly as he dared to the mound.

"How many you walked so far, Hoss?"

"Just one. I got a three to nothing count on this batter."

"Okay. You're doing fine. Don't worry about it. We just hired ourselves a new pitcher, but he's having trouble squeezing into a uniform. Big Noise is in there helping him, but it'll be a few minutes yet. Now what I want you to do is stall until he gets here."

"You want I should pitch slow, Johnny?"

"Right. Take lots of time between pitches. Go and talk things over with the third baseman. Turn around and count how many fans are in the bleachers. Untie your shoe and then tie it again. But whatever you do, do it slow."

Hoss Hill nodded. The plan suited him fine. He

liked to pitch as deliberately as possible. He liked everything about pitching, in fact, except having to throw the ball in the direction of home plate.

Hobbes strolled back toward the dugout. The fans were getting impatient. They began to clap. Dusty Hornbostel, the home-plate umpire, yelled, "Play ball!" Hill started to wind up. Then he stopped and studied the baseball. He called time out and tossed it to McBride, who handed it to the umpire.

"I guess Hoss wants a new one," the catcher said.

Dusty Hornbostel looked at the ball. It seemed perfectly all right to him.

"What difference does it make?" he demanded. "He won't get it within twenty feet of home plate anyway."

But he threw Hoss a new ball. Hill threw it back.

"Ball four," Dusty said, and St. Louis had two men on.

Hoss worked as slowly as he dared, glancing hopefully now and then at the dugout, but by the time Big Noise called time and walked out to the mound he'd walked a third man and the count was three balls and no strikes on the batter. Winnetka slapped him on the back.

"Good work, Hoss. Now you can go take a shower."

"I took one yesterday. And the day before."

"Well, go take another." He gestured toward Five-Yard, who was strolling out toward the mound. "We just got ourselves a secret weapon."

"Fuller now pitching for the Gnats," the stadium announcer said.

The voice booming over the loudspeakers startled Five-Yard. But then he grinned in pleased surprise.

"Now that's right neighborly, telling everybody who I am," he told the manager. "I only wish Ma was here to see how friendly everybody is in the big city. What you want I should do now, Mr. Big Noise?"

"You see that base over there?"

"Right in front of the fellow in the chicken-wire mask?"

"That's called home plate. I want you to stand here on this little hill—we like to call it the pitcher's mound—and throw your garter-snake outshoot over that plate and strike out the side." He clutched Fuller's arm. "You think you can do it, kid?"

"Why, sure, Mr. Big Noise. And after I've done that, what you want me to do?"

Winnetka stepped back two paces. He gazed up at the young man.

"I'll think of something," he said. "You can be sure of that."

⊖ **2** ⊖

In the broadcasting booth back of home plate, Mush-mouth Flang, the famous television announcer, was angry. Big Noise Winnetka had no right to put in a new pitcher without sending up a press kit to the booth giving the rookie's history and statistics. Mushmouth prided himself on having plenty of statistics at his fingertips. There were those who claimed Flang didn't know much about baseball, but no one could ever deny that he gave the television audience a lot more information about the players than the people wanted to know.

When a new pitcher came in, it was Flang's custom to tell the listeners what size shirt he wore, how many cornflakes he'd eaten for breakfast, what kind of a batting average he'd had when he was in the fifth grade and other fascinating information of a similar nature. Sometimes by the time Mushmouth had finished giving his listeners a rundown on the new player's back-

18

ground the game was over and it was time for the final commercial, but this didn't bother Flang a bit.

As the announcer given the unhappy assignment of describing the brand of baseball played by the New York Gnats, he felt that the thing to do was to fill the listeners so full of unnecessary information that they wouldn't have time to think about what was going on down on the field.

And now here was some overgrown kid named Fuller going in to pitch and Flang didn't have the remotest clue to his life history. He turned to his assistant, Ted Hobbes, for help.

"Well, Ted, boy, it seems that the Gnats are putting in a rookie. Fuller, his name is. Big, muscular-looking boy, wouldn't you say?"

"Yes, I certainly would," Ted said. "Yes, I would say you've hit the nail right on the old button there, Mushmouth."

"Your brother being the third-base coach of the Gnats, I suppose he's mentioned this new pitcher of theirs?"

"Well, no, as a matter of fact, he hasn't.We had dinner together over at our sister Wendy's house only yesterday and Johnny didn't say a word about it. But then he doesn't like to talk about the Gnats while he's eating."

Flang sighed. He put his hand over the microphone for a moment to shut off the sound. He told Ted to telephone down to the clubhouse and see what he could find out about this Fuller person. Then he settled back and looked out at the field, prepared to carry on as best he could.

"Well, folks, while we're waiting let's review the situation. This is the last half of the ninth with the Gnats ahead fourteen to thirteen. The bases are loaded—Hoss Hill was a little wild today—and the count is three and nothing on Hap Hawkins. Hawkins is five foot eight and a half, weighs one-eighty, and he's up there swinging a thirty-eight-ounce bat. His neck size is seventeen and the license number on his car is— But there's the first pitch. It's a—"

Mushmouth Flang stopped talking. His jaw hung open. He rubbed his hand over his eyes. He blinked them a couple of times. He leaned over to take a drink of water. His hand was trembling so he spilled most of it down his shirt front.

"It's a strike, folks," he said, finally. "Now how shall I describe it? It wasn't a screwball. On the other hand, it wasn't a slider, either. It started out like it was going to be an inside curve, but then it kind of twisted around toward the left and then it dipped back to the right and it—" He stopped. He got a firm grip on himself. "But you and I know, folks, that there isn't any pitch like that. We must have been seeing things. Now let's pay close attention this time. Everybody wake up out there. Get close to your television sets. Here's the windup. Here's the—"

He stopped. Once again his mouth was open but no sound was coming out. Five-Yard had been in big-league baseball only a few minutes, but already he had done something that a hundred thousand television watchers had been wishing for ever since the first Gnats broadcast had gone on the air. He had made Mushmouth Flang shut up.

20

Down on the field, Dusty Hornbostel flung his arm aloft. Back in the booth, the announcer finally managed to regain his voice.

"Now, folks, let's not panic," Flang croaked. "The count is three and two. That much I know. Let's hang onto that thought. That's a firm statistic. It doesn't twist around from right to left and back to right again. And now let's watch this next pitch. It's what we call the payoff pitch because the count is three and two and the bases are loaded and— But here it comes. Strike three. Hap Hawkins never moved his bat. He looks a little stunned. He's taking out his handkerchief and wiping his forehead. He's walking slowly away.

"Now there's one away and Horatio Kelley is due to bat. He was standing over there in the on-deck circle watching what was going on and now he's supposed to go to bat. Horatio Kelley is twenty-two years old, stands six foot one, weighs one ninety-two. His batting average in elementary school was two eighty-six. He wears size fourteen socks, size thirteen shoes and he— But wait a minute, folks.

"There seeems to be some difficulty getting Kelley to take his turn in the batting box. He's just standing there in the on-deck circle shaking his head. The first-base coach is running down there and arguing with him. Kelley doesn't seem to want to walk up there to the plate. The coach is behind him now, pushing. Kelley doesn't seem to want to bat against this rookie pitcher the Gnats just added to their roster."

Flang glanced over at Hobbes, but Ted was still on the phone.

"Well, while we're waiting for Kelley to make up his

MUSHMOUTH FLANG

mind, let me fill you in on a few statistics. There've been a total of thirty-six hits so far in this game, twenty-seven runs and the Gnats have made seven errors. The wind is from the southeast at six-point-three miles an hour, the temperature in Anchorage, Alaska, is forty-seven degrees and—

"But there he goes. Kelley has been shoved into the batter's box. He's getting ready. And here's the pitch. It was a strike. I'm not going to try to describe what kind of a pitch that was, folks. I'd rather let you judge for yourselves. Kelley's getting set again. He's got a funny expression on his face. Let me put the glasses on

22

him. Why, he's—I can't understand this, but I swear he's got his eyes closed. Well, anything can happen in this great game of baseball, folks, and here comes the ball and Kelley is swinging with his eyes closed and he came closer than he did last time. He only missed by a foot and a half."

Kelley had put everything he had into that swing. Now he settled back with the air of a man who has done his best and watched the third strike twist past him. Then he walked over to the bench in the dugout and sat down and put his head in his hands.

With two down and the bases loaded, the St. Louis manager decided he needed a pinch hitter. He wasn't sure just what was happening, but he knew he'd never seen a pitcher like Fuller before. He glanced down the row of ballplayers. All of them avoided his eye except Lefty Joe Rasmussen. Lefty Joe had been in the big leagues for nearly twenty years and he was no longer the star he had once been. But he'd seen plenty of pitchers come and go and he wasn't afraid of any of them. The manager nodded to him. Lefty Joe leaped to his feet and grabbed a bat. He strode up to the plate. Fuller had been standing on the mound watching a jet fly overhead, but now he looked toward home plate and stuffed the ball in his hip pocket and came trotting in, his hand outstretched. Mike McBride, with an eye on the runners, called time out.

"Say, aren't you Mr. Lefty Joe Rasmussen?" Five-Yard demanded. "Boy, wait'll I tell Ma I've seen you in person."

"What is this?" Rasmussen demanded. "Let's play ball."

"You're Ma's favorite ballplayer. She's told me about you ever since I was knee-high. She says she saw you once a few years after she and Pa was married and you hit a home run into the bleachers that bounced right over her head. Like to of scared her to death. But she said you probably didn't even know she was there, so she forgave you. Say, you wouldn't autograph this here ball for her, would you?"

"Play ball!" Dusty Hornbostel yelled. "What're you trying to pull, kid?"

"Why, not a thing. It's just that it'd make Ma awful happy if I could bring her a baseball signed by her favorite player, Mr. Lefty Joe Rasmussen. She always regretted not jumping up on Pa's shoulders and grabbing that home run he hit in the bleachers. Would you mind, Mr. Lefty Joe? I got a pen right here."

"Oh, all right," the Cardinal player said. He grabbed the pen and signed his name on the ball. "Now can we get back to the game?"

Five-Yard thanked him and walked back to the pitcher's mound. McBride crouched down behind the plate. Five-Yard noticed that the catcher was wiggling his fingers behind his mitt, so he waved back, friendly-like. Then he threw three strikes. Rasmussen swung at every one of them, his expression grim and determined, but he missed and the game was over.

Lefty Joe started back to the dugout. Fuller hurried after him.

"I sure was sorry to have to do that," he said. "But I didn't have much choice."

"That's okay, kid. You struck me out fair and square. There's no hard feelings."

24

"Well, I sure am glad to hear that. I had to do it. If you'd hit the ball it might of got all scuffed up and it wouldn't look as good on Ma's mantelpiece."

Upstairs in the broadcasting booth, Mushmouth Flang was still going over the statistics of the game for his listeners when Ted Hobbes grabbed his arm. Flang turned to him impatiently.

"You know I don't like to be interrupted when I'm giving the folks statistical information, Ted, boy. What is it?"

"I found out who Fuller is. I finally got the information you wanted."

"Well, don't just stand there. Tell the folks about it. Who is he?"

Hobbes told the audience about how Five-Yard had just been signed by the Gnats. He told them how Fuller had walked in off the farm the previous fall and joined a last-place football team, the Knights.

"I'm sure you remember what he accomplished in the pro football league last season, Mushmouth. Everybody agrees he was the main reason why the Knights won the championship."

"I knew he looked familiar," Flang said. "A football player who's switched to baseball. Now isn't that something? You didn't happen to get his statistics did you, Ted, boy? How much he weighs, what size belt he wears and interesting stuff like that? No? Well, then, I guess that winds us up for today, and after a word from our sponsor we'll— But wait a minute, folks. I do have a statistic for you after all. It has just occurred to me. It wouldn't have occurred to most announcers, but Mushmouth Flang doesn't let things like

25

this get by him for long. Folks, you've seen history being made today. You've seen a new all-time world's record set this very afternoon."

"A new world's record?" Hobbes said. "I don't see—"

"Of course you don't see, Ted, boy. But I do. Five-Yard Fuller has been in organized baseball only a half hour and already he's the holder of the world's record for the most opposing batters struck out in a single inning by a fullback."

⊝ 3 ⊝

LOSING the game to Five-Yard and his garter-snake
outshoot took something out of the Cards. During the last two games of the series with the Gnats the
St. Louis players kept glancing anxiously over their
shoulders at the New York bullpen to make sure Fuller
wasn't warming up. And while the Cardinals were
worrying about Five-Yard, the Gnats suddenly began
to look like big-league ball players. Mule Bradshaw hit
two homers and a triple in the two games. Lefty Lecos,
the center fielder, got four singles and a double. And
what pleased Big Noise Winnetka most of all, Four-
Fingers caught another fly ball. True, he forgot his
glove and grabbed it barehanded, but it made two
catches in three days for him, a new record.

The team set a record, too. By taking three games in
a row, it established its longest winning streak in five
years.

"Now we're only thirty-two games out of first place," Big Noise told Johnny Hobbes. "I know it's too early to brag, but maybe we'll finally get out of tenth. With Five-Yard pitching every fourth day, we might finish as high as ninth."

When the team got ready to leave St. Louis and head home to New York, however, the manager's dreams of future glory were smashed. Fuller said he couldn't go.

"Can't go!" Winnetka cried, turning red in the face. "What do you mean you can't go?"

"I appreciate the invite, Mr. Big Noise. But this is the busy time of year back in Rock Creek. Things going on every day—weeds to hoe, fertilizer to spread, cows to milk."

"For the amount we're paying you to throw a baseball, you could get a hired hand."

"Ma wouldn't hold still for that."

"But she lets you play for the Knights during the football season."

"She didn't want to at first, but she finally said it was okay. But in the fall, most of the chores around the farm are finished. Ma won't hold with me fooling around and playing games while there's important stuff like plowing to do."

"Think of the salary we're paying you. You'd never make that much planting buckwheat."

"Oh, Ma don't care about that. She says it's more important to be busy doing something useful than to make a pile of money."

"She wouldn't consider playing in the big leagues useful?"

"Well, now, Mr. Big Noise, I wouldn't want to hurt your feelings. But you got to admit that raising hogs or planting alfalfa is a lot more sensible work than throwing a ball around."

"I admit nothing of the kind," Winnetka shouted. "I've got your name on a contract, Five-Yard. Either you come along with us to New York or I'll send you to a farm team."

"Well, now, that's a right nice thought. I guess I'd feel right to home on a farm team. What do they raise —sorghum?"

"Never mind that. I want you in New York. I need you, Five-Yard. You're my one chance of getting this team as high as ninth."

"Oh, I'm willing to go. But only if Ma says it's okay."

Winnetka saw a ray of hope.

"Then all we've got to do is send Johnny Hobbes out there to Rock Creek, if there really is such a place, and get her to give her permission."

"But if I know Ma, she'll say no."

Winnetka considered making the trip himself, but he decided against it. After a lifetime of dealing with umpires, the only way he knew how to argue was to wave his arms and yell. Hobbes was more diplomatic.

"But what if I can't talk her into it?" Johnny asked, nervously.

"You'll talk her into it. You've got to. But if you don't, you'd better start hunting around for another job."

The nearest airport to Rock Creek was more than a

hundred miles away, so when Johnny got there he hired a helicopter. It came swooping down on the farm just as Ma Fuller was calling her husband and two older sons to supper.

Hobbes had been expecting to see a big, rawboned woman with a loud voice. When he found that Ma was small and gentle-looking, particularly in contrast to her hulking menfolks, he couldn't understand why Five-Yard let her boss him around.

"This isn't going to be as hard as I thought, Harry," he told the helicopter pilot as they climbed to the ground.

He presented Five-Yard's mother with a bouquet of red roses he had bought at a florist's shop in the city. She thanked him politely.

"I'll just put these in a water glass on the dining-room table, right next to the two dozen I picked out of the garden today," she told him.

Hobbes and the pilot joined the family in one of the finest meals they'd ever tasted. While he was eating, he made plans for what he would say to Mrs. Fuller as soon as they'd finished with the dessert. The first slab of rhubarb pie was so good that he accepted a second piece and then a third. He finally pushed himself away from the table and glanced around the room.

"Anyone seen Mrs. Fuller lately?" he asked. "I've got some important business to talk over with her."

"Ma went out in the back yard," Sylvester told him.

"She said she'd be back in a little while and you was to make yourself to home," the other brother, Leopold, added.

Harry, the helicopter pilot, came running in, waving his arms.

"My chopper's gone. Somebody's taken my chopper."

The Fuller boys grinned at each other. Hobbes ran outside with the pilot. The helicopter was gone, all right. But as they stood there in the farmyard they heard the noise of its rotors. In a moment it came swooping in over the barn. Ma Fuller waved at them from the glassed-in nose. The pilot covered his eyes with his hand.

"She's going to smash up my chopper. She's going to ruin it."

Pa Fuller strolled over. He glanced up at the helicopter. It was swooping around over their heads like a barn swallow chasing bugs.

"Now don't you fret, mister," he said. "Ma'll come down when she's good and ready."

"She'll come down, all right," the pilot said. "The law of gravity will see to that. But when she does she'll be killed and the 'copter will be wrecked."

"Oh, Ma can run your contraption all right," Fuller said.

"You mean she's a qualified helicopter pilot?" Hobbes demanded.

"Ma's qualified to do anything she sets her mind to. Of course, she's never happened to see one of these machines before, but that don't make no never mind."

The pilot started explaining how complicated it was to operate a helicopter and how many weeks of instruction were necessary before it was safe to solo. Meanwhile Ma took one final swoop around the farmyard, hovered for a few moments over the barn roof, then came spiraling down toward them.

Hobbes dove behind the woodpile. The pilot tried to crawl under the porch. But she made a perfect landing. She jumped briskly out of the helicopter and walked over to them.

"Now that's what I call downright enjoyable," she said. "I was thinking about perching on the barn roof, but I was afraid I'd scare the pigeons."

"Lady, I don't know how you did it," the pilot told her. "I just don't know how you managed to fly it without anybody showing you how."

"Oh, you men always make things sound so complicated. I been operating a foot-pedal sewing machine for years. This wasn't near as hard as making pleats."

The pilot went over and sat down with his back against a tree and started talking bitterly to himself. Hobbes decided that dealing with Five-Yard's mother might not be as simple as he'd supposed. Still, he had to try. He began by telling Ma how her youngest son had come down out of the stands to strike out the side.

"That boy's a caution," Ma said, fondly. "Always playing games. But then, he's the baby of the family. I guess one of these days he'll grow up."

"Oh, I certainly hope not, Mrs. Fuller. He has a great future ahead of him as a pitcher. I'm sure you wouldn't stand in his way. But just as a formality, I came here to get your permission for him to play with the New York Gnats."

"That's a baseball team?"

"There was some doubt about it before Five-Yard showed up. But now it's beginning to look like one."

"I did let Clarence play football last fall," Ma said. "But of course I came along to make sure he wore his rubbers and ate right."

"Oh, you'd be welcome to visit him any time you wanted. And it's a good healthy life he'd be leading— plenty of exercise in the open air. And, of course, as a pitcher he'd only have to work every fourth day unless the manager decides he needs him in the bullpen."

"He'd be good at that," Ma said. "He knows all about bulls. But I can't have him gallivanting around all summer while there's work to be done here. And I certainly don't like the idea of him working only one day out of four. Idle hands lead to trouble. No, Mr. Hobbes, I'm sorry, but I'm afraid Clarence will have to come back home where he belongs."

Johnny argued. He cajoled. He pleaded. Ma just stood there, shaking her head. Finally, he could see it was no use. She had made up her mind. There was nothing he could say that would change it. He didn't know how he was going to face Winnetka with the news.

"It would have been such a wonderful thing to get out of tenth place," he said, wistfully. "Big Noise would've been so proud to be the manager of a ninth-place team. But without Five-Yard he never will be."

"Somebody's got to be in last place," Ma told him.

"I can see I can't make you understand. I've lost the argument. But one thing you learn from associating

33

with the Gnats, Mrs. Fuller. You learn how to lose gracefully. You've had so much practice." He turned to the pilot, who was still examining his helicopter, puzzling over how Ma could have flown it. "Come on, Harry. Let's go."

"No hard feelings, I hope," Ma said.

"No hard feelings. I'll send Five-Yard home." He reached into his pocket and brought out a baseball. "I almost forgot. He wanted me to bring you this."

Ma glanced at it. Then she peered at it more closely.

"Lefty Joe Rasmussen signed this personally?" she demanded.

"Just before your son struck him out."

"Clarence got to meet him in person?"

"He certainly did. In fact, Lefty Joe will remember the day for a long time. Well, Mrs. Fuller, we ought to be starting back now. Say goodbye to your husband and the two boys for me, and best of luck to you."

"Now just you wait a minute, Mr. Hobbes. Don't go rushing off. That's the trouble with you city fellows, always in a hurry. You say Clarence and Lefty Joe would be playing together?"

"Not on the same team. But on the same field, whenever St. Louis is in town."

"Well, then," Ma said. "Why didn't you say that in the first place? I guess if Clarence is going to have a chance to associate with people like Mr. Lefty Joe Rasmussen I oughtn't to stand in his way." She gazed off across the farm yard. There was a faraway look in her eyes. "I got a powerful lot of respect for Mr. Lefty Joe. I guess you might say he's my hero. He's been my hero ever since he hit that home run I almost caught the day Pa treated me to a seat in the bleachers on our wedding anniversary."

Hobbes glanced down at her in delighted amazement. He would have sworn that Ma Fuller was blushing.

⊜ 4 ⊜

THE first game of the Gnats' home stand was with
Houston. The stadium was filled. The fans had
turned out to see their team take another licking. It
had become a pleasant pastime for them to go out to
the ball park to laugh at the collection of misfits, to
cheer when Four-Fingers dropped a fly, to feel a glow
of satisfaction when the team found a new and entirely
unprecedented way of blowing another game. But on
the sunny afternoon when the team returned to New
York to play Houston things didn't work out the way
everyone expected.

Five-Yard was the starting pitcher. For the first
eight innings the Gnats played errorless ball, mostly
because for the first eight innings no Houston batter
did anything but strike out. Standing out there in right
field, Fibich began to get restless. He had liked it better when he had more to do.

"Don't bear down so hard, kid," he told Five-Yard as the Gnats came to bat in the last of the eighth. "Let 'em hit a few. We're all behind you."

"You want to catch a few flies, Mr. Fibich?"

"That's what I'm paid for, kid. There's nothing to it. All it takes is four fingers and a thumb."

Now that Fibich had brought it up, Five-Yard could see how the rest of the team would feel kind of left out and useless if he didn't give them anything to do. So in the top of the ninth he quit throwing his garter-snake outshoot. Instead he lobbed the ball up to the plate. Sure enough, the Houston batter hit it. It went sailing out toward right field. Five-Yard pivoted to watch it.

"There you are, Mr. Four-Fingers. Just like you wanted."

Fibich was ready. He began to sprint in toward first base. Then, changing his mind, he turned and headed full tilt for the right-field wall. The ball drifted lazily down and hit the turf about twenty feet behind him. Whirling around, Four-Fingers charged at it, bending down to pick it up. He missed. He came back and fumbled around, finally coming up with it and making a wild throw toward second base just as the Houston batter came loping across home plate.

Winnetka stalked gloomily to the mound.

"Now we're behind one to nothing. But don't let it bother you, Five-Yard. Get the side out. We've still got one more time at bat."

"Oh, that didn't bother me none," Fuller assured him. "I guess Mr. Four-Fingers will feel better now he's had some exercise. I'll let the next batter hit it out to Mr. Lecos in center so he can have some fun, too."

Winnetka stared at him. "You mean you deliberately let that guy hit the last one? What're you doing, trying to throw the game?"

"Well, it didn't seem fair for me to be the only one playing. Striking out everybody, it was just like Mr. McBride and me was playing catch. I could see how the other fellows might get tired of standing around. Of course, if you'd rather I went back to striking them out . . ."

Big Noise made a mighty effort to get a grip on himself.

"Yes," he said, "I'd rather you struck them out. If you don't mind. If it wouldn't be too much trouble."

"Oh, it won't be no trouble at all," Five-Yard assured him, and struck out the side.

But now Houston was one run ahead and the lower part of the Gnats' batting order was coming up. The lower part of the Gnats' batting order was even less likely to score a run than the upper part of the Gnats' batting order, which was saying quite a bit.

Still, as Mushmouth Flang, the famous television announcer, was so fond of reminding his audience, you never can tell what will happen in the great game of baseball. Chip Woods, the Gnats' third baseman, popped the ball just over the shortstop's head and wound up on base. Satchel-Foot Mooney, the nearly immobile second baseman, hit a long fly over the center fielder's head and somehow made it all the way to first without getting thrown out. That put men on first and second with no one out and Five-Yard coming to

38

bat. Winnetka put a fatherly arm around the pitcher's shoulder.

"Now here's our strategy, Five-Yard. We can't expect to get any more hits. We never get more than two in an inning, so we've used up our quota. But if you lay down a sacrifice bunt, we might get men on second and third with only one out. Then the next batter might get lucky and hit a fly ball so the man on third could score and tie the game. Okay?"

"Okay, Mr. Big Noise. Only can I ask one question? What's a bunt?"

Winnetka explained how he should slide his hands forward on the bat and punch at the ball, laying it down along the first-base line so it would be hard to make a play at third. Five-Yard said it sounded like a real clever idea. He walked up to the batter's box but before the Houston pitcher had thrown the ball Five-Yard called time out. He strolled out to the mound.

"I don't want to do nothing sneaky, mister. Ma always taught us boys not to pull tricks on anybody, so I thought I'd better tell you. I'm going to bunt."

"What're you trying to pull?" the pitcher demanded. "I suppose you want me to think you're going to bunt and then you'll swing away."

"No, Mr. Big Noise said I was supposed to choke up on the bat and sort of punch it down toward first base. Don't you believe me?"

"Oh, sure. I believe you."

The pitcher glared at him. Then he signaled to the infield to move back, positive that Five-Yard planned to hit the ball as hard as he could. Fuller shrugged. He'd done his best. He couldn't help it if the Houston pitcher was suspicious. He stood in the batter's box practicing how to slide his hands forward on the bat the way the manager had showed him. While he was practicing, the Houston pitcher threw two strikes past him. He decided he'd better concentrate on the game.

Over on the bench, Winnetka smote his knee in disgust.

"Now the count's two and nothing," he told Johnny Hobbes. "He won't be able to bunt because it's the third strike. Why is life always so difficult?"

"You're the manager of the New York Gnats," Hobbes told him, feeling that this was explanation enough.

"Say, do you suppose he realizes you're not supposed to bunt on the third strike?" Big Noise demanded, jumping to his feet.

But it was too late to do anything about it. The pitcher had thrown the ball. Five-Yard's hands were choking the bat. He was lunging at the ball. The manager groaned.

But it didn't go foul. The bat met the ball squarely. Five-Yard had aimed it down the first-base line, all right. But he had hit it harder than he'd intended. The ball went sailing over the first baseman's head and bounced to the fence. By the time the outfielder had picked it up and thrown it back, two runs had scored, Five-Yard was on third and the Gnats had won the game.

Hobbes pounded Winnetka on the back.

"You know what this means, Big Noise? We're in ninth place. For the first time since you've been manager the Gnats aren't trailing the league."

"It's the day I've dreamed of, Johnny. But there's one thing wrong."

"What's that?"

"Now that we've finally got to ninth, I'm not satisfied. I want to go higher. I want to go as high as eighth."

Hobbes looked over toward third base where Five-Yard was standing.

"I suppose we're dreaming. But I have the feeling that it isn't impossible, at that."

In the dressing room, the other players clustered around Fuller, congratulating him. Five-Yard shook his head and went gloomily off to find the manager and tell him he was sorry.

"Sorry? What for?"

"For not doing like you told me. I was trying to bounce it down the first-base line and make an out, but it's the first time I ever did any of that bunting stuff and I didn't do it right. Next time I'll try to do better."

But Winnetka wasn't a man to hold a grudge. He said that as long as Five-Yard had won the game by bunting to the right-field wall, he'd forgive him.

⊖ 5 ⊖

WITH the season half over, the Gnats had climbed into eighth place, a mere twenty-seven games out of first. This unaccustomed height in the standings was due mostly to Five-Yard, although now and then the team won without him on the mound. There was the game, for example, when Lefty Lecos stole home with the winning run because he saw Winnetka scratching his ear and thought it was the signal for a suicide squeeze. (Actually, the manager's ear itched, which seemed to him sufficient reason for scratching it.) Then there was the night game where Four-Fingers lost the ball in the lights and accidentally caught it, surprising the opponents so much that they let the Gnats win.

But mostly the rise in the standings was due to Fuller and his garter-snake outshoot. The nine opposing managers in the league began to worry. Jojo Johnson of the Braves was one of them. He called a council

42

of war before his team opened its series with the Gnats. He demanded whether anyone had any ideas about how to deal with Five-Yard.

"Why don't we refuse to show up at the ballpark on the day he's due to pitch?" No-Nose Schmidt said. "You don't know what it's like, trying to bat against that kid. You see that curve ball of his darting back and forth and you know your eyes must be playing you tricks. You know it can't be doing what you see it doing. While you're thinking about it, you hear it smack into McBride's mitt and you've struck out again. It's downright humiliating."

"I'm not interested in hearing why you can't hit his outshoot," Jojo said. "I'm interested in finding a way to change things. Now I want you fellows to watch this movie."

"I hope it's one with Doris Day," No-Nose said. "I like Doris Day movies."

Jojo looked at him in disgust. He explained that the movie had been made secretly with a telephoto lens concealed in a bratwurst bun held by a spy stationed behind first base. It was a scientific study of Five-Yard's pitching. Some of it was in slow motion to help them see what the ball did.

"Hey, that's a great idea," Schmidt said. "If we could get him to use slow motion, we might get a hit once out of every ten times."

The group settled back. The lights went out. For the next fifteen minutes, the men watched in horrified silence as the garter-snake outshoot twisted its way from Five-Yard's hand to the catcher's mitt. Occasionally, the cameraman had focused on the batters' faces, which always wore the same expression of deep astonishment. When the lights came on again, Jojo looked around the room. Even No-Nose, who was usually full of optimism, was gloomy.

"I like horror pictures," he said. "But this one was too much for me. I kept thinking how I got to go out there tomorrow and strike out."

"Didn't any of you guys get a clue?" Jojo asked. "What were the batters doing wrong?"

"They weren't doing anything different than they always do," the third-base coach said. "They were holding their hands right. They were keeping their eyes on the ball."

"Watching the ball, the way Fuller throws it, only confuses you," No-Nose Schmidt said.

Jojo jumped to his feet. "That's the first thing I've ever heard you say that makes sense. Maybe that's the answer we've been looking for."

"What is?"

"Maybe the thing to do is to discard all the traditional rules of batting. Instead of watching the ball, for instance, maybe it'd be better just to swing at it without looking. According to the law of averages, you'd be bound to hit it by accident once in a while."

"Just close your eyes and swing," No-Nose said. "A great idea. I'm sure glad I thought of it."

It seemed like a forlorn hope. Still, no one could come up with anything better. When the Braves went out on the field to play the Gnats the following afternoon with Fuller on the mound, the batters were ordered to swing without looking. No one got a hit for several innings, but Jojo grimly stuck to his strategy.

44

In the fifth, one of the Braves connected for a double. In the sixth, another batter hit a long fly to Lefty Lecos that might easily have been a hit. The score was still nothing to nothing, but the Braves manager was encouraged.

"We're starting to get to him, boys. Keep in there swinging. And keep your eye off the ball."

In the eighth, the strategy paid off. No-Nose Schmidt, his eyes tightly closed, gave a mighty heave of the bat. The ball went soaring into the stands. Winnetka hurried out to the mound to talk with his pitcher.

"They're starting to hit you, boy."

"Gee, I'm sorry, Mr. Big Noise. That's the first run anybody's scored in the last seven games I've pitched. I don't know what went wrong."

"You're not easing up, are you?"

"Nope. I'm pitching just the same as always."

Winnetka took off his cap and ran his hand over his bald head. He'd been afraid of something like this, he said. The garter-snake outshoot was a great pitch, all right. But after the batters had seen it often enough they were bound to figure it out. The thing to do was to mix up the pitches more.

"Throw a fast one once in a while, Five-Yard. That way, when the garter-snake comes in, they won't always be expecting it."

"You want me to rear back and let 'er fly as hard as I can?"

"That's the idea."

"You think Mr. McBride'll be able to catch it?"

"Mike's one of the best catchers in baseball, kid. You

45

don't have to worry about him. Give it all you've got."

Five-Yard nodded, but he still looked a little doubtful. The next batter was waving his bat. The umpire was looking impatient. Fuller waited until the manager was off the field. Then he coiled himself into a knot and threw.

None of the three men around home plate moved. The batter still stood there, looking menacingly out at the pitcher. Mike McBride was still crouched down, waiting. The umpire, Bo Bliffert, was still peering over the catcher's shoulder.

"Excuse me, Mr. Bo," Five-Yard said, politely. "But was that a ball or a strike?"

"Was what a ball or a strike?"

"Why, the ball I just now threw."

"You threw the ball? I didn't see it. I saw you bring your arm down, but that's all I saw."

"I didn't see it either," the batter said.

"If you threw it, where is it?" McBride demanded.

Five-Yard pointed to the backstop. The ball was imbedded in the heavy wire netting. Mike turned pale.

"You mean that whizzed by me? How am I supposed to catch something I can't see?"

"I don't know what you're complaining about," the batter said, backing away from the plate, his right leg trembling so hard he had to steady himself with his bat. "At least you've got a mask and chest protector, Mike. Standing up here without one while he's throwing his fast ball is the next thing to suicide."

"I may decide to resign, myself," Bo Bliffert said.

"Are you sure you aren't trying to pull some kind of trick? How do I know you really threw it?"

"Oh, I'd be glad to do it again," Five-Yard said. "I guess we better have a fresh ball, though. There isn't much left of the old one."

The batter got set again. The umpire braced himself. McBride crouched down. Five-Yard wound himself up like a clock spring and let fly. The ball appeared as if by magic, imbedded in the netting.

"What was it?" Five-Yard asked. "Ball or strike?"

The umpire opened his mouth a couple of times before anything came out. Then he croaked: "Ball two." McBride started to give him an argument.

"How can you possibly know, Bo? None of us saw it go past."

"Any time I don't see it go over the plate between the batter's shoulders and his knees, it's a ball, isn't it? I'm warning you that every one like it is going to be called the same way."

The batter walked on four straight. He took second on the first passed ball, went to third on the next and came home on the pitch after that. By this time, McBride had had enough.

"I've been lucky so far," he told Five-Yard. "I haven't caught any of them. Can't we go back to the good old garter-snake?"

"But Mr. Big Noise said I ought to mix my pitches up."

"Well, mix in some outshoots, buddy. Otherwise I'm going to demand extra combat pay for working where the bullets are flying."

Five-Yard could see how upset the catcher felt, so

47

he went back to his triple curve. The Braves didn't score again. But neither did the Gnats and the game was lost. As they were leaving the dressing room, Fuller ran into Hoss Hill, who told him not to look so downcast.

"But I feel like I've let the team down," Five-Yard said.

"Everybody loses one now and then. Even me. What does that make your record now—eight and one?"

"Something like that, I guess."

"Don't let it bother you. That's about the same as the best record I've had in the major leagues, and I've been around a lot longer than you."

"When'd you ever have an eight-and-one record, Hoss?" Hobbes demanded.

"Well, I didn't say our records were identical. I just said they were about the same. Five-Yard has eight and one and my best year I had one and eight. Same figures, only turned around. But one thing you've got to admit. When I throw the ball, McBride can catch it."

"If he can reach it, he can," Johnny said. "But usually he has to stand down near first base to do it."

⊝ **6** ⊝

THE CUBS were next. By the time they arrived in town, word of the Braves' success with Fuller had percolated through the league. The grapevine had carried word of how it had been done.

"Don't keep your eye on the ball," the Cubs' players were ordered.

Winnetka knew the talk was going around. He was worried. If Five-Yard quit winning, the team would sink down into tenth place again. It had dropped three out of four to the Braves, including Fuller's loss in the opener. For a while, Big Noise had been allowing himself to hope that the team might climb into the first division, but now he'd settle for staying in eighth. Even doing that well with a team like the Gnats ought to qualify him for election as manager of the year. He decided to have a talk with Fuller. He told him to forget about his fast ball.

"It doesn't do any good to throw strikes if the ump can't see them. But I still think you ought to mix up your pitches. Can't you come up with something else?"

"Like what, Mr. Big Noise?"

"Oh, maybe a change of pace—you know, when they're expecting a curve you throw them a slow one. The batters are mostly swinging with their eyes closed now anyway, so it might be pretty effective."

"I never tried that change of pace, or whatever you call it. Is it anything like the yoyo pitch?"

"The what?"

"The yoyo. I used to use it sometimes back home when we'd choose up teams. The boys that used to play in back of the schoolhouse in Rock Creek had trouble hitting it."

"Well, I don't know. I never heard of a pitch like that. You've got to remember that the Cubs are major leaguers."

"Those fellows I used to play with back of the schoolhouse were pretty good, too. There was Seth Cameron, who worked at the feed store, and Soupbone Welch, who ran the filling station, and then there was Crazy-Legs Walfoort, who—"

"Never mind. I'll try anything once. Go ahead and use your yoyo, whatever it is. But maybe you ought to wait until we get a lead before you experiment."

Bearing that advice in mind, Five-Yard began to wonder if he'd ever have a chance to try his new pitch. The Cubs went ahead in the third inning when Skeeter Ferrara booted an easy grounder into left field, where Sandy Dunes picked it up and threw it over Mule Bradshaw's head, letting the batter run all the way around the bases on what should have been an out. Mike McBride got a hit in the fifth but was out at second when Lefty Lecos missed the signal for a hit-and-run play.

"Didn't you see me scratching my ear?" Winnetka demanded. "That meant you were supposed to swing away."

"Oh, I saw you all right," Lecos said. "But I just figured your ear must be itching again."

Satchel-Foot Mooney hit a single in the seventh inning, but was left stranded on first. Then in the eighth, with the Cubs still ahead one to nothing, the Gnats finally came alive.

Four-Fingers Fibich started things off. He hit a mighty fly ball toward right field. He glanced up. His expert knowledge of fielding told him that the ball would be caught, so he strolled slowly down toward first base, his hands in his pockets. When he finally realized that the ball was over the fielder's head, he began to run. He took a long turn around first and began to head for second, but his batting helmet fell off. He stopped to pick it up, fumbled it a couple of times, and just barely managed to dive back headlong into first ahead of the ball.

That gave him a single on what should have been a triple and put the tying run on base, with Mike McBride at bat. The catcher popped one over the infield, reaching first. Fibich stopped at second. Lefty Lecos walked, filling the bases with no one out. Dunes was up next.

"Just a long fly ball, Sandy," Big Noise ordered. "I don't expect a hit. Just give us a long fly."

53

Things seemed to be going well for a change. Winnetka stood in front of the dugout, watching. A mosquito landed on his left ear.

"Get out of here, friend. I got trouble enough with Gnats without having to worry about mosquitoes."

He slapped the side of his head with his open hand. The blow hurt him more than it did the mosquito. He began to rub his ear vigorously. Taking a long lead off first, Lecos saw the gesture.

"It doesn't make much sense," Lefty muttered to himself. "But he's the manager. He must know what he's doing."

He took off for second in a cloud of dust. Mike McBride, who was already there, regarded him with horror.

"No room!" he yelled. "Get back!"

Fibich, on third, saw what was happening. He ran over toward second to give Lecos the benefit of some advice.

"Go back to first, Lefty," he yelled.

"Go back yourself," McBride told Four-Fingers. "What's going on here, anyway?"

The Cubs pitcher wondered the same thing. He stood holding the ball. He couldn't understand why all the Gnats' base runners had suddenly decided to have a convention at second base. Duke King, the Cubs' second baseman, took command.

"Wake up, there. Throw me the ball."

The pitcher obeyed. Duke grabbed it. He whirled around, trying to decide which runner to tag first. He picked McBride.

"You're out."

"Not me, Duke. I'm standing on second."

King saw he'd made a mistake. He lunged at Lecos. Lefty had finally concluded that the manager's signal had been wrong. He started scrambling frantically back toward first base. Duke ran after him. McBride turned to see Four-Fingers still standing near second, watching the action.

"Don't you think you ought to get back to third?"

Fibich could see the logic of the suggestion. He took off for third. Duke, sensing the movement behind him, turned and threw the ball to Kiki Moriarity, who wasn't expecting it. He grabbed it and jammed it into McBride's chest.

"I'm still standing on second," Mike pointed out. "I haven't moved a muscle."

"Throw it to third," Duke yelled.

Moriarity did. But the third baseman had run over behind second, on the theory that it was there the action was, so there was no one on third to catch it. Four-Fingers ran home and McBride took third.

Lecos wound up on second.

"It was where I was planning to go all along," Lefty explained later.

That tied the game. Dunes flied out to the center fielder, permitting McBride to score, and when the inning ended the Gnats were leading, two to one.

"Can I try my yoyo pitch now, Mr. Big Noise?" Fuller asked as the Cubs came to bat in the ninth.

"Go ahead. But if it doesn't work, go back to the garter-snake before they score."

Five-Yard nodded. Kiki Moriarity, who was leading

55

off for the Cubs, took his place in the batter's box. Fuller called time and went in to talk with him.

"I'm going to quit throwing outshoots for a while, Mr. Moriarity. I figured it was only fair to let you know."

Kiki regarded him suspiciously. So, for that matter, did Mike McBride.

"Now look here, Five-Yard," the catcher said. "I'm not going to stand back of the plate if you're going to start throwing that invisible fast ball again."

"Me, either," said Sunny Max Shapiro, the umpire. "If you're planning to start throwing it, tell me and I'll go find some safer line of work, like jumping off bridges."

"Oh, I'm not going to throw the fast one. I just thought I'd switch over to my yoyo for a while, if you don't mind."

"What's this about a yoyo?" Kiki demanded. "I thought we was supposed to be playing baseball. Next thing you know we'll be playing marbles or spinning tops."

"Say, that sounds like fun," Five-Yard said. "But I guess we ought to get this game over with first. The thing is, I wanted to give you a chance to get ready for my yoyo pitch."

"I'm as ready as I'll ever be," Kiki said. "Let's get it over with so I can go back to the bench and sit down."

Up in the announcer's booth, Mushmouth Flang was taking advantage of the lull in the game to give his fans some statistics. He was a little annoyed when Five-Yard strolled back to the mound and took his windup because it meant he had to watch the field again.

56

Mushmouth liked to talk about baseball, but he didn't care much about watching it. Something was always happening down there on the diamond that he was supposed to explain.

"Well, folks," he sighed, "here we go again. The Gnats are leading two to one and Kiki Moriarity is at bat. Fuller is taking his windup and here's the pitch. It's what he calls his garter-snake outshoot, a sort of triple curve which— But wait a minute. He crossed me up. Did you see that, Ted, boy? He didn't throw his outshoot. What would you say that pitch was?"

"It was a strike," Ted Hobbes said. "Sunny Max Shapiro called it a strike."

"I know it was a strike, Ted, boy. I saw the ump hold up his hand. I'm not blind. Or am I? I saw the ball come down toward home plate. Then I saw it stop and reverse itself and head back toward the pitcher. Then I saw it change direction again and go across the plate. And finally, just as McBride was reaching out to catch it, it reversed itself once more and darted back to Fuller's glove. Is that what you saw too, Ted, boy?"

"I thought that's what I saw, Mushmouth. But obviously I couldn't have. There isn't any pitch like that."

"You're absolutely right, Ted, boy. I happen to be a student of the great game of baseball and I know there isn't any pitch like that in the record books. And if it isn't in the record books, it isn't so. Just disregard that pitch, folks. We'll pretend it didn't occur."

Down on the field, McBride looked in amazement at Sunny Max Shapiro.

"What happened?"

"How should I know? I'm only the umpire. All I can

57

be sure of is that I saw the ball come over the plate, so I called it a strike. But then I saw it scoot back to the pitcher again."

"Then shouldn't it be two strikes? It went over the plate twice."

"Don't get me any more confused than I am."

"I didn't see it," Kiki Moriarity said. "I swung with my eyes closed, the way the manager ordered."

"You're better off," Shapiro told him. "I may start umpiring with my eyes closed, too. Then I won't get nightmares from seeing things no umpire is supposed to have to see. I'm not going to sleep very well tonight, I can tell you."

"I guess that's why he calls it his yoyo pitch," McBride said, "because it behaves like it was on a string. Shall we try it again?"

"I'm game·if you are," Kiki told him. "This time I think I'll keep my eyes open and watch. It sounds interesting."

Five-Yard wound up and threw. The ball shot full speed toward the plate, stopped about a foot away, headed back toward the pitcher's mound, reversed itself again and crossed over the plate. Moriarity was regarding the ball in fascinated astonishment. McBride kept his hands at his side, making no move to catch it. He didn't need to, for just before it reached him the ball headed back to Five-Yard.

"This is a threat to the catching profession," McBride said. "It's made the catcher obsolete."

"I guess that must have been strike two," Sunny Max said. "Or maybe strike four, if you want to count it going in both directions."

"Let's just call it strike three," Kiki Moriarity said. "I'm glad I saw that pitch once. It'll give me something to tell my grandchildren. But I'd just as soon not have to see it again. Now all I want to do is go back in the dugout and lie down."

⊖ 7 ⊖

Aᶠᵀᴱᴿ Moriarity had struck out, the Cubs went through the motions of finishing the game, but without much enthusiasm. The Gnats' losing streak was broken. So were the spirits of the opposing teams. The Gnats swept the series with the Cubs. They took three out of four with Los Angeles. They won the first three with the Giants and would have won the fourth except that an easy fly ball was hit toward Four-Fingers Fibich with the bases loaded, and naturally that gave San Francisco four runs. When St. Louis came to town, the Gnats had climbed all the way to fifth place.

"The first division!" Winnetka said. "I never thought I'd live to see the day."

"Fuller's responsible," Hobbes reminded him. "Even when he isn't pitching, the other teams are worrying about him. They had troubles enough when all he threw was the triple outshoot. Now that he's using that yoyo pitch, too, they don't have a chance. Besides, winning a few games has inspired the rest of the team. They're starting to play good baseball, at least part of the time."

"Fuller makes that ball do tricks I never thought were possible," the manager said. "How do you suppose he does it?"

"I'd rather not know."

"But my curiosity's aroused. It looks like magic, but there's got to be some natural explanation. I won't rest until I find out what it is."

"Do you think you ought to, Big Noise? Things are going so well. Why rock the boat?"

"I'm the manager. I've got a right to know why my star pitcher can make the ball do things it's never done before. But when even a great scientist like Dr. Wernheim von Schwandfelter can't tell how—"

"You hired Dr. von Schwandfelter to watch Five-Yard?"

"Secretly, from along the third-base line. I figured as long as he was the world's most famous physicist he ought to be able to find out how the kid makes a round object—the baseball—move back and forth or stop in midair."

"If anybody could, he ought to be able to. Has he turned in a report yet?"

"All he turned in was his resignation. After watching Five-Yard, he took the first plane back to Vienna. He wrote me a letter from there."

"What did it say?"

61

"I've got it right here in my pocket. You can read it yourself."

Winnetka handed the crumpled sheet of paper to Hobbes. The writing was hard to read—Dr. von Schwandfelter seemed to have been rather shaky when he wrote it—but Johnny finally figured out what it said.

"It is obviously impossible for a ball to do the things I saw it do," he read. "Fuller has broken all the laws of physics. Keep your money. No one will ever know how he does what I saw him do."

Hobbes said he guessed that settled the matter—if von Schwandfelter couldn't figure it out, no one could. Winnetka agreed.

"Still, I'd sure like to know how he makes the ball do those tricks," the manager said. "If we knew, maybe we could develop a pitching staff where everybody had his own yoyo pitch. Imagine what that'd do to baseball."

"Have you ever thought of asking Five-Yard how he does it?"

"What does he know about physics?"

"It wouldn't hurt to try."

Winnetka said it was a foolish idea. Still, the next time he saw Five-Yard, he asked him anyway. Five-Yard said it was all very simple.

"Simple! A renowned scientist like Dr. von Schwandfelter can't figure it out, and you claim it's simple."

"Why, sure. All Dr. von What's-his-name had to do was to ask me. I'd of been glad to of explained it to him."

"You know more about physics than he does, I suppose."

"It don't have nothing to do with physics. It's farming that did it."

"Did what?"

"Gave me this semicircular callus between the first and second fingers of my pitching hand. It comes from holding the plow, pitching hay, cleaning out stalls and stuff like that. I've had this here semicircular callus ever since I was a sprout."

The manager grabbed Fuller's hand to take a look. Sure enough, there was a large callus on the side of his middle finger. It was shaped like a new moon.

"When I throw the garter-snake outshoot, I grip the ball so the callus touches the underside of it. That gives it a double reverse back-spin. When I throw my yoyo, I stick the ball between my two fingers, with the callus kind of on top. That starts it whirling in one direction for a while, then in the other direction. It makes the ball come back toward me like it was on a string."

"You mean anybody could pitch like you if they had a callus like that?"

"Well, they'd have to be pretty strong, too. They'd have to be able to throw the ball pretty fast. What I do, I throw the other pitches like I do my invisible fast ball, only the spin the callus puts on it slows it down enough so people can see it. If I didn't have the callus, all I could throw would be the fast one. On that one, I don't use the callus. I just rear back and let 'er go. And then Mr. McBride misses it."

Winnetka glanced anxiously around to be sure no one had heard.

"Don't ever tell anybody your secret, Five-Yard. If the other managers ever hear about it, they're liable to pass a rule against it or something. Don't breathe it to another soul."

Fuller promised he wouldn't. But later, thinking it over, Big Noise felt he just had to tell somebody. What was the use of knowing a secret if he couldn't share it? It was such a good joke on the other managers—all the anguish they were having in trying to figure out how to beat Five-Yard was caused by something as simple as a plowboy's callus. He finally decided he would tell his wife. His wife told her best friend, swearing the friend to secrecy. Within twenty-four hours, the news had spread from Los Angeles to Philadelphia.

As soon as the other nine managers heard about it, they called strategy sessions. Lights burned late in hotel rooms. The best brains in organized baseball sought a solution to the problem of how to cash in on their new knowledge. Fats Indigo, the San Francisco manager, was the first to figure out an answer. He called a midnight meeting of his entire pitching staff. He asked them how many of them would like to be able to pitch like Five-Yard. Every hand was raised.

"Okay, then. Here's what I want you to do. On the days when you're not pitching baseballs, I want you out in the country pitching hay. And the first one to get a semicircular callus on the middle finger of his pitching hand gets a fat bonus."

The Giants' pitchers were not enthusiastic about going into the hay fields, but Fats Indigo gave them no choice. He got them up at 6:00 A.M. the next day, pointing out that no farmer is supposed to stay in bed past sunup, and sent them out in the countryside to apply for jobs. It took them quite a while to find a farmer who still used hand labor instead of machines to harvest his hay crop, but finally they found one whose tractor had broken down. He was willing to let them pitch hay as long as they didn't expect any pay for it, he said. The Giants' pitching staff went to work. Each day, a couple of them would go back to the stadium—one to start the game, the other to work in the bullpen in case a relief pitcher was needed. The others kept hard at work in the hay fields, from sunup to sundown.

"I don't know," Snub Shirer said after a few days of this. "I'd like to be able to pitch like Five-Yard, but this hard labor is killing me. The reason I went into baseball was so I wouldn't have to work for a living, and now look what happens. I got half a mind to tell Fats I won't do it."

"And get fined and suspended?" Bobby Catton said. "He didn't give us much choice. You getting a callus yet?"

"Nope. But I've got one of the finest collections of blisters in the United States."

"Me, too. And my arm's so stiff I can't raise it. Do you suppose this is really the best way to improve our pitching?"

"Fats must know what he's doing," Snub said. "At least, I hope he knows what he's doing."

By the time the Gnats arrived in San Francisco for their four-game series, there wasn't a pitcher on the Giants' staff who could walk from the dugout to the mound without groaning with every step he took. Some of the Giants' pitchers couldn't throw the ball as far as home plate. Those who could were so lame from all their unaccustomed exercise that the ball came floating up with nothing on it. Even the kind of batters who played for the New York Gnats found they could get hits. In fact, in the opening game, with Five-Yard pitching, the final score was twenty-one to nothing. It would have been higher except that the Gnats got tired of running around the bases and started deliberately striking out so they could go back to the hotel and eat dinner.

The Gnats swept the series. In Los Angeles, where the pitching staff had copied Fats Indigo's methods, they won all four games. In Houston, the same thing happened. By now it was obvious to all the managers that sending their pitchers to pitch hay had been a serious mistake. The experiment was quickly stopped. But the lame arms persisted for a while. In the first two weeks after Fats got his idea of how to grow calluses, the Gnats lost only one game. Tommy Scott of the Giants shut them out. He explained afterward that when his manager had sent him to pitch hay he'd gone fishing instead, thus escaping the epidemic of sore muscles.

Gradually the blisters healed and the aching arms got well again. But by then the Gnats were in third place, a mere ten games out of first. As the plane headed back to New York, Big Noise relaxed in his seat and grinned at Johnny Hobbes.

"What a road trip this has been. This'll show those sports writers who claimed this was the worst team in the history of organized baseball."

"And they were right, until Fuller came along,"

Hobbes said. "He's made all the difference. If something should happen to him . . ."

Winnetka shuddered at the thought.

"Don't say things like that, Johnny."

He turned to Bananas Entwhistle, the club's public relations man. "Do you suppose I ought to get a speech ready for the crowd?"

"What crowd?" Bananas said.

"Surely there'll be a crowd of joyful fans to greet us at the airport. Why don't you write me a short speech, full of pride and modesty, telling how I discovered Five-Yard and gave him the benefit of my advice, making him into the greatest pitcher the game has ever seen."

But the speech wasn't needed. No one showed up at the airport to welcome them home from the most successful road trip in the team's history. The next day, when the home stand opened, the stadium was less than a quarter full.

Four-Fingers Fibich, who was accustomed to hearing the laughter of the crowd when he tried to catch a fly ball, felt lost and lonely out there in right field with no one jeering at him from the stands. He got to brooding about it. He was so preoccupied, in fact, that when one of the Philadelphia batters hit a line drive at him he reached out his gloved hand and caught it. A couple of diehard fans sitting along the first base line threw their bags of salted-in-the-shell peanuts down in disgust and got up to leave.

"A guy just can't depend on anything any more," one of them told the other. "Not only do the Gnats quit losing and start behaving just like every other ball team, but Four-Fingers starts in catching flies. I thought we could at least depend on him to keep up the team's tradition."

"You said it, Al," his companion agreed. "I came out here to enjoy myself watching the Gnats make fools of themselves. If I'd wanted to watch good baseball I'd have tuned in the Yanks on the TV."

The Gnats won the opener behind Fuller. They lost the second game of the series, then took the next two. But the attendance was so small that Bananas Entwhistle went storming into Winnetka's office and told him he'd have to do something about it.

"Fuller's spoiling our public image," the press agent shouted.

Winnetka regarded him with astonishment.

"How can you say that? He's got a nineteen-and-one record with a third of the season left to play."

"Sure, sure. But did you see how many empty seats there were today? And yesterday. And the day before that. The thing is, Big Noise, our fans had more fun watching the games when the Gnats were losing. They paid their money to come out and see what stupid trick the boys would pull next. For a couple of bucks, a guy could buy a ticket and sit there feeling proud and happy. He figured even he could do better than the kind of players we had on the field. But now the team's starting to play good baseball and its public image is spoiled."

"Four-Fingers misjudged one today," Winnetka pointed out.

"Sure. But then he grabbed the ball and threw it to second in time to get the runner. In the old days, he'd

68

have thrown it to first so the runner could have gone to third. Things just aren't the same since Fuller joined the team."

"You're right," Winnetka said, leaning back in his chair and glaring at the press agent. "You're certainly right. And I, for one, am glad of it."

"You won't send Five-Yard back to Rock Creek then, I suppose."

"No, I won't. Because do you know what's going to happen to the Gnats? We're going to win the pennant. As long as Five-Yard's arm holds out, we're going to climb all the way to first place. And then we're going to win the World Series. And I don't care if nobody comes out to watch us, because all of a sudden I'm managing a real baseball team."

Bananas Entwhistle looked at the manager in disgust.

"You're dreaming, Big Noise. Sure, Fuller's a great pitcher. But the rest of the guys are playing over their heads. They'll go back to being the clowns they always were and you'll go back to managing a tenth-place team. The Gnats win the pennant! They've got as much chance of winning the pennant as you have of getting elected governor of the state."

After Bananas had gone, Winnetka walked over to the mirror in his office. He studied his profile. He decided he wouldn't make a bad-looking governor, at that.

8

"THE trouble is, there's nothing to do here in New York," Five-Yard said. "I miss Rock Creek."

He was standing in the manager's office, looking thoroughly miserable. Winnetka had noticed that his star pitcher was troubled about something and had called him in to find out what it was.

"You're homesick?" Big Noise asked.

"I guess you might say so. I've tried not to be. I decided the best thing to do was make the best of things so yesterday I got a bamboo pole and some angleworms and went fishing in the East River, down at the foot of Wall Street. But I didn't catch a thing. Not even a crawdad. Then I went over to Central Park and asked one of the hired hands there if I could hoe the flower beds."

"My best pitcher handling a hoe—I hope none of the sports writers saw you."

"Oh, I never got ahold of the hoe. This hired hand said I had to pass a civil service exam first. Back home, you don't have to pass no test to swing a hoe."

"I might let you mow the center-field grass with a scythe if it'd make you happy," Winnetka suggested.

"It wouldn't be the same as back home. Sometimes I wake up in the middle of the night in that fancy suite you rented for me in the hotel and wish I was back on the farm, where I could go out and pound fence posts or slop the hogs. It makes it hard for me to keep my mind on my pitching."

The manager jumped to his feet in alarm.

"Don't you dare let anything take your mind off that, Five-Yard. If you ever quit pitching the Gnats would fall right back down in the cellar again."

"And another thing, Mr. Big Noise. All that fancy cooking in the hotel dining room—it don't hardly stick to your ribs at all. Now if I could just get me one of Ma's home-cooked meals—"

"But Pierre is one of the finest French chefs in Manhattan."

"Then how come he never cooks stuff like turnip greens or fried hog jowls? You take a good mess of turnip greens, with plenty of fatback drippings poured on top, and—"

"You're making me ill, Five-Yard. Forget about things like that. Start thinking about how you're going to win forty games for us this season."

"I'll sure try, Mr. Big Noise. But I don't know how much longer I'll be able to keep up my strength without Ma's cooking. If she was here—"

Winnetka put up his hand. If that was what it took

71

to keep his best pitcher happy, he said, he would charter a helicopter and send it to Rock Creek to pick up Mrs. Fuller and bring her to New York. She would be there in time for the game tomorrow.

Five-Yard looked so happy that the manager decided the expense would be worthwhile, especially as it was the club's money he planned to spend to hire the helicopter.

The following morning, the bubble-topped machine settled down in the Fuller farmyard. Ma Fuller put on her Sunday bonnet and climbed aboard.

"I hear on the party-line phone that my baby boy needs me in the big city," she told the pilot. "So naturally I'm all ready to go. Now if you'll just shove over—"

"But lady, I'm the pilot. I'm supposed to sit here in the pilot's seat."

"Nonsense and folderol. I know you men drivers, always taking chances. Either I run this contraption or I get out and walk."

The pilot put up quite an argument, but he lost. Somehow men always did lose arguments with Ma Fuller. Somewhat to his surprise, they missed the barn roof when they took off, although they did bend one of the lightning rods a little. Ma Fuller flew low over the feed store to wave to some of her friends. Then she pulled back the throttle and headed for New York. The pilot made one final protest.

"You don't have a license to fly this machine. You'll get in trouble with the United States government."

"I'd just like to see some whippersnapper try it," Ma Fuller told him. "Now hang on tight. Let's see if we can loop the loop like I used to see Richard Barthelmess do in them movies about World War I."

While Ma and the frightened pilot were flapping their way toward New York, Five-Yard was in the Gnats' stadium ready to face the Braves. He was looking so happy before the game that Four-Fingers Fibich asked him why.

"I won't have to eat that filet mignon and stuff like that any more," Five-Yard told him. "Ma's coming to take over the cooking for the team. Isn't that great?"

"She's a good cook?"

"I'll say. You don't know what good cooking is till you've tasted her squashed cucumber pie with chocolate sauce."

Fibich turned pale.

"Sounds like quite a change from Pierre. What else does she plan to feed us?"

"Oh, you never can tell about Ma. She's always coming up with something new. Like the time she whipped up a mess of collard greens with salt pork, then mixed it all together with stewed woodchuck gravy and added a dash of horseradish to bring out the flavor. Even Pa admitted he'd never tasted anything like that before."

Four-Fingers wiped his forehead. He was turning slightly green around the eyes.

"I don't feel very well, Five-Yard. All of a sudden, I feel kind of sick."

"Gee, that's too bad. I wish Ma was here. She'd give you a good dose of pie plant and milkweed tea and you'd be ready for a big meal of chopped calves' brains in no time at all."

73

Fibich stared at him. He started to say something. But then he clapped his hand over his mouth and ran toward the dugout. Johnny Hobbes, who had been walking by, asked Five-Yard where the outfielder was going in such a hurry.

"I guess all that talk about Ma's cooking must of made him hungry," Fuller said. "It sure did me. I could eat a horse—if Ma cooked it, that is. What time'll she be here?"

"She's on her way, that's all I know. You ready to beat these guys today?"

"I sure am. I feel great, knowing Ma's coming. I was thinking I might celebrate by using my dogleg pitch."

Hobbes looked at him suspiciously. He'd never heard of a pitch like that, he said. Five-Yard said not many people had.

"Describe it for me."

"Well, you know how a dog's hind leg is shaped—it starts out in one direction, then kind of switches around and goes in the other. That's how this pitch goes. Even Crazy-Legs Walfoort used to have trouble hitting that one when we used to play ball behind the school."

Hobbes was still doubtful, but he decided to let things take their course and see what happened. No-Nose Schmidt led off the first inning for the Braves. He crouched low in the batter's box and pounded the plate with his bat.

"Come on, country boy," he yelled. "I'm going to hit it right down your throat."

"I'd kind of hate to have you do that, Mr. No-Nose. I guess I better try my dogleg pitch on you. Are you ready for it?"

"I'm ready for anything, country boy," Schmidt shouted, pounding the bat on the plate again.

"Well, I'm not," Mike McBride said. He called time and hurried out to the mound. "What's this new pitch?"

"Well, if you see me wind up and look like I'm throwing the ball toward Mr. Mule Bradshaw over at first base, be ready to catch it."

"You mean it starts out toward first and then whips over home plate?"

"You catch on fast, Mr. McBride. That's why I call it the dogleg pitch. You ever happen to notice how a dog's hind leg—"

"Never mind the scientific explanation," the catcher said. "I guess if No-Nose can stand it, I can. He's the one who's got to try to hit it."

McBride walked back and crouched nervously behind home plate. Schmidt picked up a handful of dirt, wiped his hands on his shirt, then got set in the batter's box, scowling ferociously at Five-Yard. Fuller took his windup, then sent the ball toward Mule Bradshaw. No-Nose whirled to protest to Dusty Hornbostel, the umpire.

"What's he trying to do, pick a runner off first when there isn't any runner?"

"Strike one," Hornbostel replied, waving one arm aloft.

"Strike! But he threw it to first."

"That's what you think," McBride said, tossing the ball back to Five-Yard. "Next time why don't you watch what's going on? You might find it interesting."

Schmidt did watch. He watched the ball start out toward Bradshaw, then make a sharp turn and come streaking across the plate. He watched Dusty Hornbostel's arm go up, signaling another strike. He watched all this happen, but he didn't believe his eyes. Even after he had struck out and was back in the dugout, he didn't believe them.

Five-Yard felt so good about the prospect of soon seeing Ma Fuller and eating her cooking that he threw nothing but strikes for the first six innings so the game would end sooner. He mixed up his pitches, switching from the dogleg to the yoyo to the garter-snake outshoot, then back to the dogleg again. After the Gnats had scored two runs in the bottom of the sixth, No-Nose Schmidt came to bat again in the top of the seventh, grimly determined to get on base. When the ball came whipping toward the inside the corner of the plate, he leaned forward enough so that it brushed his sleeve.

"Take your base," Hornbostel bawled.

"He did that deliberately, ump," McBride protested.

"Don't argue with the umpire," Dusty ordered, and No-Nose trotted down to first, grinning triumphantly.

"Us old pros know more than one way to get on base, country boy," he shouted to Five-Yard.

He took a short lead. He watched Fuller take his stretch and throw his first pitch to the next batter. As the ball started toward home plate, No-Nose ran a few steps toward second. But when the ball got halfway to home, it changed direction. It came zipping over to Mule Bradshaw, who grabbed it and tagged the runner out.

"I'm sorry to do that, Mr. No-Nose," Five-Yard told him. "But I'm in kind of a hurry to get this game over. I used my reverse dogleg that time."

76

"Go ahead and laugh, country boy. I just hope I get to bat once more. I'll hit that ball if it's the last thing I ever do."

Five-Yard switched to his fast ball against two of the Braves' batters and walked them. He went back to his other pitches in time to get the side out. With one man out in the ninth, Schmidt came up again. Schmidt had been giving Five-Yard's pitching considerable thought and he had a plan.

"I bet you can't strike me out with your yoyo pitch, country boy," he yelled.

"Ma doesn't hold with us betting, Mr. No-Nose. But I'll throw you a yoyo if you want me to."

"Don't do it," McBride ordered. "He's got something up his sleeve."

"Afraid I'll hit it if I know what's coming?" Schmidt demanded.

"We're not afraid of a thing," Mike said. "Go ahead, strike him out with the yoyo, Five-Yard."

Fuller took his windup and threw. The ball paused a few feet ahead of home plate, started back toward the pitcher's mound, then reversed direction again and headed across the plate. No-Nose watched it go, not moving a muscle. But then, when the ball reversed direction once more and headed back toward Five-Yard, Schmidt gave a mighty swing. There was a loud crack as the ball met the bat. The ball headed on a mighty arc toward the center-field bleachers.

"A homer," No-Nose shouted, and began trotting toward first base.

But the ball never reached the bleachers. As it sped in that direction, a helicopter came fluttering over the

stadium wall. Ma Fuller reached out through the window and grabbed the ball. Then the machine swooped in and hovered a few feet above the pitcher's mound. She tossed the baseball to Five-Yard.

"Here you are, son. I was afraid if I let it go it'd get lost and you'd have to stop your game."

"Oh, we got another ball, Ma. But thanks anyway. Have a nice trip?"

"Fair to middling, son. Who's that red-faced fellow running out toward us? Maybe he wants to thank me for bringing back the ball."

"That's Mr. Dusty Hornbostel, Ma." He turned proudly to the umpire, who came storming up, waving his arms. "Mr. Dusty, I'd like you to make the acquaintance of Ma."

"Pleased to meet you," Ma yelled down.

But Dusty wasn't very polite. He waved his arms some more.

"Get that whirlybird out of here, lady," he shouted. "You think this is an airport or something? Get that thing off my field."

"Now don't go getting your dander up, mister," Ma told him. "I was just trying to do you all a favor, returning your ball. Besides, I'm not on your field. I'm a'setting up here twenty feet above it."

"It's against the rules, having some crazy dame in a helicopter hovering over the pitcher's mound. At least, it ought to be against the rules."

No-Nose had completed his run around the bases. Now he demanded to know whether the run counted. Hornbostel said it did.

80

"The ball didn't go out of the park," McBride protested.

"It was interfered with by a spectator, so I say it's a homer."

"You show me the ground rule that says a ball caught by a player's mother while flying a helicopter over the center-field bleachers is considered a home run," Mike said.

"Can you show me a rule that says it isn't?"

"Oh, let it count," Five-Yard said. "I want to get this game over with so I can go get me a home-cooked meal. Ma, maybe you ought to move up a couple of hundred feet. You're making Mr. Dusty nervous."

"Why, sure, son. I can see he's getting even redder in the face. He looks just like those people on the Empire State Building did a few minutes ago. I just buzzed by to say hello, friendly-like, and they got all shook up."

Ma took the helicopter farther up in the air and Five-Yard struck out the side to end the game. He was so hungry, thinking about Ma's cooking, that he was glad when it ended. Dusty Hornbostel had no appetite at all, but he was glad when the game ended, too.

"Women drivers," he muttered after he had called the final strike. "Even in the middle of a baseball diamond they follow me. I wish I'd taken up some other line of work."

⊝9⊝

With Ma taking over the cooking for the Gnats, Five-Yard was his old cheerful self again. He pitched so well that whenever he started a game it was as good as won. The rest of the team members were a little doubtful about their change in diet. But it turned out that whatever Ma cooked was delicious, providing they didn't ask questions about the ingredients.

Ma grumbled a little about how backward and behind the times New York grocery stores were. She said she couldn't find the makings for a pot of possum-liver soup and she'd had trouble finding a supermarket that stocked extract of rutabaga oil. However, being a good cook, she made do with the things she had and everybody on the team began to gain weight, including Big Noise Winnetka, who had been trying for years to lose a few pounds.

"Clean up your plate," she kept telling him. "Clean up your plate or you won't get any of my chokecherry pie."

"But I'm not supposed to have any dessert, Ma."

"Now don't be modest and hang back, Big Noise. You'll waste away with only two helpings. Clean up your plate again. Then you'll be big and strong so if you ever lose your soft job as manager and have to go to work for a living you'll be ready."

In spite of Five-Yard's pitching, the Gnats couldn't seem to climb higher than third. A month or two before, Winnetka would have been delighted to settle for this respectable altitude in the standings. But now he was dreaming of bigger things.

"I might pitch Five-Yard every day, just until we get into first place," he suggested.

"And maybe ruin the kid's arm?" Johnny Hobbes demanded. "We don't want to overdo a good thing and spoil it."

"But I'm worried about what'll happen to the team when the football season starts and Five-Yard has to leave to play for the Knights. They signed him up first, you know. I want us to get far enough ahead before that happens so we can manage without him."

"I still say he can't pitch oftener than one day out of three or four," Hobbes insisted.

"Then what am I supposed to do? None of the other pitchers can hold the opposition to less than five or six runs. And with the kind of hitting I'm getting from the team, that means we aren't winning more than a third of the games that Five-Yard doesn't pitch. If we only had one really good hitter it might be different."

"Excuse me, Mr. Big Noise," Five-Yard said. "Could I make a suggestion? Why don't you put me in to pinch hit?"

"Now wait a minute, kid. You're the best pitcher I've ever seen or ever expect to see. But do you know what your batting average is? Except for that one time when I told you to bunt and you pushed the ball all the way to the fence, all you've ever done is stand up there at the plate with your bat on your shoulder."

"I've been meaning to ask about that, Mr. Big Noise. I been wondering if it mightn't be better for me to swing at the ball once in a while."

"What's stopping you?"

"I figured as long as you didn't tell me to swing, I wasn't supposed to. I didn't want to step out of line."

"You mean to tell me you've been waiting all this time—" With an effort, Winnetka got a grip on himself. "Of course I want you to try to get hits, Five-Yard. That's the way the game is played. Swing all you want to—not that I expect anything special in the way of hitting from a pitcher. Most pitchers can't hit a lick."

"Oh, I used to hit pretty good back of the schoolhouse. Why don't you put me in now? While we been talking here on the bench we've got two men on base. I could go in and bat and knock them in. That is, if you wanted me to."

Winnetka looked at Hobbes, who shrugged.

"If he says he can do it, he probably can," the coach said. "Besides, what've we got to lose? Satchel-Foot Mooney's up next. He's so slow that unless he hits the ball all the way to the wall he gets thrown out at first."

84

Mushmouth Flang, in his glassed-in booth behind home plate, was startled to hear the field announcer tell the crowd that Fuller was batting for Mooney.

"Well, folks, you can never tell what's going to happen in this great game of baseball," he reminded the television audience. "Here is Fuller, who has had only one hit this year, going in to bat for Mooney with two men on and two men out and the Gnats behind by one run. The only explanation I can think of is that Big Noise Winnetka has flipped his lid. Now while we're waiting for Five-Yard to take his place in the batter's box, let me fill you in on some statistics. Fuller wears a size fourteen shoe, a size nine and a half hat, and while he was pitching for the Rock Creek Falcons in the Three Old Cat League he had an earned average of point-eighty-two. But there's the first pitch, folks, and Five-Yard is taking a swing at it. I've never seen him take a full swing at the ball before, but you can never tell what will happen in this great game of— Wow!"

"Did you see that, Mushmouth?" Ted Hobbes demanded.

"I said 'wow!' didn't I, Ted, boy? Where would you say that ball went, exactly?"

"Well, Mushmouth, I may be wrong, but as near as I could tell the main part of the ball went over the center-field bleachers and the cover of the ball lit up there in the top row."

"I think you have analyzed the situation perfectly, Ted, boy. In fact, you might say he knocked the cover off the ball with one mighty swing of his bat. Would you say that, Ted, boy?"

"If I were as addicted to clichés as you are, I certainly would, Mushmouth. Yes, I certainly would say he swatted the ball high and far and scored a round-tripper with one poke of the stick."

"And I'd be willing to make one more observation," Mushmouth said. "I'd be willing to go on record as saying that Fuller is a pretty good hitter, for a pitcher."

It was the longest home run ever hit in the Gnats' stadium, as far as anyone could tell. No one ever found where the main part of the ball hit. The ball's cover was caught by Kermit C. Bast, a tourist from Orwell, Ohio, who was sitting in the top row of the bleachers. Kermit C. Bast framed the cover and hung it in his recreation room, where everyone admired it. Everyone, that is, except Mrs. Kermit C. Bast, who didn't like baseball very much.

After the game was over and the Gnats had won, Big Noise Winnetka called a meeting of the team in his hotel suite.

"Gentlemen," he said, "I hope that what happened today is a lesson for all of us. By a daring bit of strategy, I managed to win the game today by putting in a pitcher as a pinch hitter. But never mind telling me it was a stroke of genius. I admit it was, but now let us go on and figure out how to win the rest of the games this year."

"We ought to let Five-Yard bat more often," Johnny Hobbes said.

Winnetka glared at him. "I was going to suggest that myself. It was my idea, exactly. A hitter like that has got to play every day."

"But he can't pitch that often," Satchel-Foot Mooney said.

"Who says he has to pitch all the time? This kid can do anything—with my advice, of course. He'll take his regular pitching turn and the rest of the time he'll play somewhere else. Lecos, you haven't had a hit in three weeks. I think I'll give you a rest and let Fuller play center."

"I'd just as soon rest as not," Lefty said. "But do you suppose he can play the outfield? Can he catch a fly ball?"

Winnetka tilted himself back in his chair and put his feet on the coffee table.

"If we tell him he's supposed to, he will. We have to remember to tell him. Otherwise, he might think it was impolite or something. But I'm convinced of one things, boys. Given a little fatherly advice from a brilliant manager like me, there's nothing Five-Yard can't do."

San Francisco was playing the Gnats the next day. The game didn't start out well. The Giants got three hits before anyone was out and before the first inning ended they were ahead four to nothing. Five-Yard was third in the Gnats' batting order. Winnetka had put him there in the hope that he would come up with men on base, but neither Skeeter Ferrara nor Mule Bradshaw got a hit.

"What you want me to do, Mr. Big Noise?" Fuller asked.

"Go up there and hit the ball."

"I kind of figured you'd want me to do that. You want me to hit it any special place?"

"Over the wall would be nice. If it wouldn't be too much trouble."

"Oh, it wouldn't be no trouble. The thing is, though, I sort of promised Ma I'd hit it into Row Seven, Seat Eight in the right-field stands. She's sitting out there to watch the game. Would that be okay?"

"Sure, Five-Yard. Only you've got to remember the Giants have one of the best pitchers in the league going for them today, Si Scholl. He might have something to say about where you'll hit the ball."

"Well, I guess I'll just have to ask him, then." Five-Yard grabbed a bat and strolled out to the mound. "Is it okay with you if I hit the ball into Row Seven, Seat Eight of the right-field stands?" he asked, politely. "It'd give Ma a chance to try out that glove she borrowed from the clubhouse."

"I'd rather you didn't," Si told him. "If it's all the same to you, I'd rather you struck out."

"But then Ma wouldn't get a baseball souvenir."

"I'll tell you what I'll do, Five-Yard. I'm sure your mother is a fine woman. You just go ahead and strike out and after the game I'll give you a baseball for her. I'll even autograph it for her."

"Now that's right neighborly, Mr. Si. Only I'd rather you autographed this one you're holding now. Then I'll hit it to Ma."

Scholl threw his glove to the ground. He told Five-Yard he didn't mind a little kidding, but this was too much.

"Now you've made me sore. I'm going to make you go down swinging at nothing but air."

"Then you wouldn't mind just writing your name on

88

this here ball, would you, Mr. Si? As long as you're so sure I won't hit it."

Scholl grabbed the pen and scrawled his name on the ball. Then he stood glaring at Five-Yard's back as Fuller ambled up to the plate. The pitcher shook off a couple of signals. Then he wound up and threw. The ball whistled past Five-Yard's chin, barely missing it. The umpire started out toward the mound to warn the pitcher, but Fuller told him not to bother.

"I guess I made Mr. Si mad and the ball got away from him," he said. "I'm sure he won't do it again."

The next pitch came toward Five-Yard's ear. He moved his ear out of the way.

"It slipped again, I guess," he said. "But he's getting too close. I think I'd better hit the next one."

The count was now ball two. Scholl wound up and let fly. The pitch was high and inside again. Five-Yard leaned back, then swung. The ball went sailing out into the right-field stands. He had miscalculated slightly. The ball went into Row Nine instead of Row Seven. But by jumping on the shoulders of the man ahead of her, Ma managed to make a fine one-handed catch.

There were two runners on base the next time Five-Yard came up, so his second homer of the day tied the score. But when he came to bat again, the Giants' pitcher decided to keep the ball out of his reach. He gave him an intentional walk.

Big Noise hurried over to the first-base coaching box and called time out. He motioned to Five-Yard.

"Now if I scratch my ear, I want you to run."

"You're afraid you've got something catching?"

"No, no. That's a signal. If I scratch my ear, it means I want you to head for second. But if I touch the brim of my cap, I want you to play it safe."

"Now that's downright clever," Five-Yard said, and walked over to take his place on base.

Four-Fingers Fibich was the batter. He swung at the first pitch and missed. Fuller was so busy admiring the mighty swing that he forgot to watch Big Noise. Then he suddenly remembered that he was supposed to look for a signal.

"Did you happen to notice whether Mr. Big Noise scratched his ear?" Five-Yard asked the Giants' first baseman. "If he scratches his ear, it means I'm supposed to run to second."

"Oh, I see. Well, now that you mention it, I did see him scratching it. So I guess you'd better run. But first I want to go over and talk with the pitcher. You don't mind waiting a minute, do you?"

"Nope. I'll be right here when you get back."

The first baseman called time and ran over to tell Si Scholl about the conversation he'd just had with Five-Yard. The pitcher regarded him scornfully.

"You think he'd tell you he was going to run if he really planned to?" Scholl demanded. "You're even dumber than he is."

"I don't know, Si. He sounded awfully sincere."

"He sure had you fooled," Scholl said, laughing. "Now go back and watch for a bunt. There's nobody out."

Si was still laughing at the first baseman when he made his next pitch. As the ball left his hand, Five-Yard took off for second. The Giants' catcher grabbed the ball and threw it, but Fuller slid in safely. He stood up and dusted himself off.

"That was fun," he told the second baseman. "I hope Mr. Big Noise lets me run some more. Let me know if he starts scratching his ear, will you? If he does, that'll mean I'm supposed to steal third."

The second baseman called time. He hurried over and told the pitcher he'd just learned what signals the Gnats were using.

"Fuller told you, I suppose," Scholl said.

"That's right. If Winnetka scratches his ear he's supposed to run."

"Well, he doesn't fool me twice. He just says that because he thinks I'm too smart to believe he's telling the truth. But we'll get him this time. You go back and tell him you saw Big Noise giving the signal. Then when he takes a good lead, I'll whirl and throw you the ball and we'll pick him off."

The second baseman did as he was told. Five-Yard thanked him politely. Then he took off for third just as Scholl pivoted on his heel and threw to second. The second baseman relayed the ball to third but Five-Yard got there first.

Four-Fingers Fibich called time. He stalked out to talk to Five-Yard.

"I wish you'd quit fooling around out here. I'm getting tired of standing around watching you run the bases. Just stay put now and I'll hit you in."

"That's a good idea," Five-Yard said. "That'd put us one run ahead. Mr. Big Noise would like that. Are you going to hit the next ball pitched?"

"You can count on it. The count is two and one so

Si's going to have to come in with a fat pitch. I'll really give it a ride."

"You think I ought to wait here on third and see if anybody catches it?"

"Nobody's going to catch it when I hit it," Four-Fingers assured him.

Five-Yard thanked him for the information. It made base running a lot simpler when he didn't have to stand around and wonder what was going to happen next. He decided as long as Fibich was going to hit the next pitch, he might as well run as soon as the ball left Scholl's hand. So when the pitcher threw, Five-Yard dashed toward home plate.

Four-Fingers had every intention of keeping his promise. He gave a mighty swing that would certainly have sent the ball over the wall if he'd hit it. He didn't hit it, though. He missed by a foot.

The catcher grabbed the ball and lunged toward Five-Yard, who hadn't bothered to slide because he'd assumed Four-Fingers would get the hit he'd promised. The catcher and Fuller collided with a crash that could be heard in deep center field. The catcher bounced back about ten feet. The ball flew out of his hand. The umpire spread his hands in the gesture that showed Five-Yard was safe. Fibich looked at his teammate in disgust.

"I'm certainly glad you're finally through running around those bases," he said. "Now maybe I can take my turn at bat in peace."

Five-Yard hurried over and picked up the catcher, who had sunk to the ground, and apologized for running into him. Then he watched as Fibich struck out and the next two batters went down in order. But it didn't matter. The Gnats were ahead, five to four, and Hank Beethoven, the New York pitcher, managed to hold the lead for the rest of the game. In the dugout, after it was over, Winnetka clapped Five-Yard on the back.

"A great job of running out there, kid. But whatever gave you the idea of stealing bases?"

"Didn't you scratch your ear?"

"I certainly didn't."

"Gee, that's funny. The Giants' first baseman said you did, so I stole second. Then the second baseman said the same thing, so I ran to third. I guess they must of made a mistake."

"They made a mistake, all right," Big Noise assured him. "And I'll bet they're sorry for it. Do you realize that we're now in second place, only five games out of first? And two whole weeks of the season left."

☻ **10** ☻

THE only team ahead of the Gnats now was the Cardinals, and New York had six games left to play with them. There was a three-game series in St. Louis. Then, after playing the Braves, Pittsburgh and the Cubs, the Gnats would get another crack at the league-leaders during the final three games of the season, when the Cards would play in New York. For a team that was trying desperately to climb higher than second place, it seemed like a favorable break in the schedule. In fact, when Big Noise Winnetka went to bed the night before the opening of the series in St. Louis, it seemed to him that everything was going his way.

But early the next morning, he found that his problems had only begun. Coach Murray Ding of Five-Yard's football team, the Knights, was pounding on the door. Winnetka put on his slippers and a bathrobe and went drowsily to open it.

"I came to get my fullback," Ding announced.

"He isn't here," Big Noise said, trying to shut the door again. "Go away."

"Don't give me that stuff," Ding said, pushing his way into the room. "I've been reading about my star back, Fuller, playing on your baseball team. I didn't mind. I figured the exercise would do him good. But now it's time for the football season to start and I've got to have him back."

"You can't have him. I've got him under contract."

"So have I. And I signed him first, so he's mine."

Big Noise pulled his robe around him and sank down on the unmade bed. He had been expecting this moment, but he had tried not to think about it. Now that the time had come to give up Five-Yard, the thought of having to play out the season without him was more than he could bear.

"Be reasonable, Ding. You don't know what it's like to manage a team like the Gnats and finally find yourself out of last place."

"But I do know. The Knights were the worst team in pro football until Five-Yard came walking across the fields from Rock Creek last fall and said he'd heard we needed a hired hand. We needed him, all right. He took us straight to the championship."

Winnetka felt faint stirrings of hope.

"Then you do understand. You know what Five-Yard has meant to us. You wouldn't have the heart to take him now, would you? After the end of the baseball season, he's all yours. Unless we win the pennant, that is. In that case, we'll need him for the World Series."

"I need him right away. Our season's starting."

"Can't we work out something? I'm willing to compromise."

"I'd be willing to compromise, too, if I didn't have him signed to a prior contract. You don't have a leg to stand on, Winnetka. I'm sorry, but I'm afraid you're out of luck."

"Then tenth place, here we come," Big Noise said.

Murray Ding was not an imaginative man and no one had ever accused him of being sentimental. But the stricken look on Winnetka's face touched his heart. After all, he had known what it was like to be in charge of a team that was a chronic loser and the laughing stock of its league.

"I know I'm going to be sorry for this," he said. "But let's see if we can work something out."

Winnetka jumped to his feet. He would have put his arms around Ding if Murray hadn't backed quickly away.

"I'll do anything," Big Noise said. "Just as long as I can have Five-Yard."

"You can't have him on Sunday afternoons, because that's when we play our games. But maybe he can play baseball the rest of the week if we can figure out some way to shuttle him back and forth."

"Wonderful. But are you sure you're willing to do that? What about your practice sessions?"

"Five-Yard doesn't need to practice. He never bothers much with signals. If the quarterback hands him the ball, he takes it down across the goal line and if somebody gets in the way he knocks him down. Football's a very simple game, the way he plays it."

"Then I accept your offer, Murray. And you'll never know how much I appreciate it."

"I have a pretty good idea. The truth of the matter is, I'm a Gnats' fan myself. I've been coaching an underdog team so long that I just naturally started rooting for those rinky-dinks of yours."

Sitting there in Winnetka's hotel room, the two men compared schedules and decided that Five-Yard would have to miss only a few of the remaining baseball games. Big Noise said he would take care of the travel arrangements.

"The club has leased a helicopter, and we can use that. We have one of the finest pilots in the country on our staff. A woman. In between times, she can continue to take care of the cooking for the team."

Ding jumped to his feet.

"I only need one guess—Ma Fuller."

"You know her?"

"I certainly do. Some of the sports writers claim she's responsible for our winning last fall, although of course they don't realize how much my coaching helped. It doesn't surprise me a bit to hear she's flying a helicopter. It wouldn't even surprise me to hear that she's flying without a helicopter or wings or anything else."

"She's a licensed pilot now. I explained to her that she shouldn't set a bad example for the boys by doing anything illegal, so she went down to Washington and had a talk with the federal aviation people. She came back and said she'd told them a thing or two and they gave her a license."

"I don't wonder. They probably were glad to get her

out of town before she landed on top of the Washington Monument."

"Oh, she did land there," Big Noise said. "She claimed it was the only place she could find to park."

Before the conference was over, the manager and the football coach were good friends. Winnetka invited Ding to come out and watch the afternoon's game from the dugout.

"Five-Yard's going to pitch. You wouldn't want to miss that."

"I sure wouldn't. Let's go."

Five-Yard ran over and grabbed Ding's hand when they got to the stadium. He started asking for news about Moose Walpurgis and his other old friends on the Knights. The coach explained how he and Big Noise had agreed to share his services.

"That is, if it's okay with you, Five-Yard. It'll be a pretty rough schedule, playing baseball all week and football on Sundays."

"Oh, that's nothing like as busy as I used to be in haying season. Besides, Ma always says a boy oughtn't to sit around or he'll get in mischief."

"Then that's settled," Big Noise said. "Now let's go out and beat them today, Five-Yard. If we win, we'll be only four games behind. If we could sweep this series, we'd be only two out of first place."

"Don't you worry, Mr. Big Noise. We'll win."

"Don't try to do anything new, now. Just your usual pitches."

"What are they?" Ding inquired. "I've been reading a lot of conflicting reports on the sports pages."

"Nothing fancy," Big Noise said. "He's got this triple

curve that acts like a garter snake with a gander after it. Then he's got the yoyo pitch, which acts like he's got the ball on a string. And now he's added the dog-leg, which starts out for first base and winds up over home plate. All very simple stuff—providing you happen to be built entirely of muscle and have a plow-boy's callus on your finger."

"A plowboy's callus?"

"It's the secret of his success. Show Murray your callus, Five-Yard."

Fuller grinned and held out his hand. Ding peered at it. He shook his head.

"I don't see anything."

"Why, it's right here, Mr. Ding," Five-Yard said, pointing with his other hand. Then he looked more closely at his finger. "That is, I thought it was here. It's gone."

"How can it be gone?" Big Noise shouted. "Who'd steal a callus?"

"You can see for yourself. It isn't there. I'd been noticing it was getting smaller, and now it's gone altogether. It must be this soft life I been leading. I got the callus in the first place from holding a plow and swinging a scythe and things like that. After a whole summer of doing nothing but tossing a baseball around, I guess it's just naturally disappeared."

Winnetka turned pale. He gripped Five-Yard's arm.

"You can still pitch, can't you?"

"I can try, Mr. Big Noise. But without my callus, I don't know whether I've anything left but my fast ball. On that one, I just rear back and throw."

"But McBride can't catch it. Worse, the ump can't

see it. Come on, boy. Let's see if things are as bad as they seem."

Winnetka called Johnny Hobbes, who grabbed a mitt and stood behind home plate. The manager ordered Fuller to try his dogleg pitch.

"Okay. Only somebody ought to stand on first, so I can get the range. It don't seem natural throwing the dogleg without Mr. Bradshaw over there."

"I'll be Bradshaw," Winnetka said, walking over to the first-base bag. "Now just forget about that callus. Just pretend it's still there. Wind up and throw your dogleg, just like you've been doing it."

Five-Yard wound up and let fly. The ball headed toward first. But instead of making a sharp turn when it got halfway there, it kept going straight at Big Noise. He barely dodged out of the way in time.

Five-Yard tried it again. The same thing happened. He tried a third time. The ball caught Big Noise on the belt buckle, moving him back several feet. The manager started groaning. Fuller ran over to him.

"You hurt, Mr. Big Noise?"

"Not really."

"Then how come you're moaning and groaning?"

"I'm thinking how hard it's going to be to win the pennant with a dogleg pitch that goes straight as an arrow. Let's try the garter-snake."

But the garter-snake outshoot didn't curve. The yoyo didn't work, either.

"I should've let you go back home between games and do your chores," Winnetka said. "I can see that now. But I suppose it's too late. How long does it take to grow a plowboy's callus?"

102

"I don't rightly know. That one took me practically all my life, I guess. I was out helping Pa in the fields since I was a little sprout."

"Then the Gnats are finished," Winnetka said. "We'll go through the motions. We'll play out the season. But we're finished."

"What's all this folderol?" Ma Fuller asked. She had come out on the field to see what was going on.

"Five-Yard's lost his callus."

Ma looked up at her son fondly. "That's the way boys are," she said. "Always losing things. Does it really matter, though?"

"Oh, no," Winnetka said, bitterly. "It just means we won't get the pennant, that's all."

Ma patted him on the shoulder.

"And you did have your heart set on getting the pennant, didn't you? Well, don't you fret. I'll get it for you."

"You will!"

"Why, sure. I was sitting in the stands the other day and there was this kid coming around, selling stuff."

"What's that got to do with it?"

"Why, he had all kind of pennants. The next time I see him, I'll buy you one."

☻ 11 ☻

WITH Five-Yard no longer able to pitch, the other teams in the league found new hope. The Cardinals won the first game of the series with the Gnats, putting them six games ahead. The Giants, who were in third place, a game back of the Gnats, started making plans to spend second-place money after the season was over. As the Gnats' players filed into their dugout before the second game of the series in St. Louis, the atmosphere was full of gloom.

"Don't give up, fellows," Five-Yard told them. "We've still got a chance."

"With our best pitcher playing center field because he can't pitch any more?" Lefty Lecos said. "What's the use of kidding ourselves? We'll be lucky if we can stay in the first division."

"He's right," Hoss Hill said. "If I could only get the ball over the plate. . . . But everybody knows I can't. I never have."

"We're a rinky-dink team without Five-Yard pitching," Four-Fingers Fibich said. "I'm supposed to be a major-league outfielder and I can't catch a fly ball."

"I thought you said all it took was four fingers and a thumb," Five-Yard reminded him.

"With me, it takes four fingers, a thumb and a bushel basket."

"You think you're bad—and you are," Satchel-Foot Mooney said. "But look at me. I can catch a ball if it's hit straight at me. But I'm so slow I can't pick up a grounder that's hit two feet to my right or left. And I'm such a slow runner, I have to hit the ball off the wall to get a single."

"It isn't that you don't try to run, Mr. Satchel-Foot," Five-Yard said. "It's just that you run too long in the same place."

"I still say we're a rinky-dink team," Four-Fingers repeated, shaking his head gloomily.

"What kind of talk is this, fellows?" Five-Yard demanded. "Ma always says if you poor-mouth yourself, you can't win."

"The guys are just being realistic," Skeeter Ferrara told him. "You're the one who got us as high as second. And now you aren't able to pitch and you won't even be able to be in center field on the days you have to play football."

"The worst of it is, we've spoiled our public image," Bananas Entwhistle said. "In the old days, we were such a poor team, people came out to laugh at us. Then, when we started to win, we lost most of our old fans. Now that people think we've got a chance at the pennant, the crowds are starting to come out again.

But when we lose, they'll be so disgusted they'll give us up for good."

"I hear the owners are talking about firing Big Noise if he doesn't manage us to a championship," Chip Woods said. "Then what can he do? Nobody'll give a job to a man who's identified with the New York Gnats."

"That settles it," Five-Yard said. "We've got to win."

"How?" Fibich asked.

"By scoring more runs than the other team. Ma's been studying the game and she was telling me that she's figured out that's all you have to do. Just score one more run than the other fellows."

"You know something?" Fibich said. "That isn't as dumb as it sounds. We haven't got any decent pitching staff without Five-Yard's callus. But we've got a good bunch of hitters. If Five-Yard knocks a home run every time he's up and the rest of us get a few singles and doubles—"

"We could give the Cards a little competition, at that," Lecos agreed.

Mule Bradshaw slapped Fuller on the back.

"If Five-Yard isn't giving up, then neither am I," he declared. "Let's go out there today and give Hoss Hill a fifteen-run lead."

"And if you do, I'll try to hold it through the bottom of the first inning," Hoss promised. "And then you can score another fifteen runs so I can get through the second."

It didn't work out quite that way. The first two Gnats' batters struck out, which brought up Five-Yard.

Catfish Carp, the St. Louis pitcher, took a long look at the large young man swinging the big bat at the plate. Then he gave him an intentional walk. Mule Bradshaw, who was up next, popped out to the shortstop and the side was out.

Hill walked gloomily to the mound. Taking careful aim at home plate, he threw the ball into the stands. His next pitch went halfway between first and home. His third hit the dirt and bounced over the catcher's head. After he had walked the first two batters without coming within twenty feet of the plate, Big Noise stalked out to the mound.

"This sort of thing has got to stop, Hoss. Isn't there some way I can persuade you to put one in the strike zone?"

"I'm trying. It's just that I get nervous with all these people watching."

"Pretend they aren't there."

"I try, but they keep yelling and making noise. I wish I was back home, pitching for the town softball team. I used to have good control then. Never walked a man."

"That's hard to believe."

"It's true. I got every pitch right over the plate. Of course, I was tossing them underhand."

Winnetka regarded him speculatively.

"Maybe that's our answer."

"You want me to throw underhand, like a softball pitcher?"

"What've we got to lose? At least they won't get to walk to first base. They'll have to hit the ball. Once in a while, maybe some fielder will accidentally catch it."

Hill did as he was told. The St. Louis batter was so startled when the ball came floating over the plate after being thrown underhand that he forgot to swing. But on the next pitch, he was ready. He hit it high and far toward center field. The runners took one look and started to scamper around the bases. Five-Yard, who had been playing shallow, turned his back to the plate and headed toward the bleachers as fast as he could go. He obviously had no chance to catch the ball. Sitting in his television booth, Mushmouth Flang could have told him that. But no one was close enough to Five-Yard to tell him he was wasting his energy and so he kept galloping along, covering an amazing amount of ground with his long legs. As he got to the wall, he turned around and jumped. The tips of his fingers barely touched the ball but somehow he hung on to it.

Then he wound up and threw it toward the infield. Satchel-Foot Mooney found it whizzing toward his glove at second base before he realized it was on its way. He grabbed it, though. He stepped on second. Then he threw it to first to double up the other Cardinal runner.

"A triple play!" Big Noise cried, slapping Johnny Hobbes on the back so hard he knocked him off the bench.

"That ought to take some of the steam out of the Cards' attack," Hobbes said after he got his breath back.

It did seem to slow St. Louis down a bit. With Hoss

Hill still pitching underhand, the Cards scored only one run the next inning and two the inning after that. Meanwhile, the Gnats were swinging hard when they had their turn at the plate. Mike McBride had a homer with two on in the third, tying the score. Then in the fourth, the pitcher got careless while he was trying to walk Five-Yard and got the ball too near the plate. Five-Yard reached out and smashed it over the wall, putting the Gnats ahead four to three.

Ma Fuller, who was sitting on the bench with the players, decided it was time to give the manager the benefit of some advice.

"Why don't you put a new pitcher in?" she asked. "Somebody who can strike out the side. That way the other team won't make any runs."

"An excellent idea," Big Noise agreed. "There's only one trouble. I don't have any pitchers like that."

"How about Mr. McBride? He must get tired having to hunker down behind home plate all the time. It'd be nice to let him pitch for a change."

"But he's a catcher."

"Could he be any worse than the pitchers you've got?" Ma asked. "Besides, I don't think it's fair, him having to keep his back turned to the crowd all the time. If I was the manager—"

"I only wish you were," Big Noise said, throwing his scorecard down in disgust.

He stalked off into the dugout to get an aspirin. His head had started aching with the first pitch of the game and it was getting no better. Ma turned to the players.

"Say, that's right nice of Mr. Big Noise to let me

manage," she said. "Now here's what I want you boys to do—"

"I didn't hear him say anything about you managing," Johnny Hobbes protested.

"He certainly did. I heard him say plain as day he wished I'd do the managing. Now Mr. McBride, I want you to go out there and pitch. And Mr. Hoss, you can do the catching. Turnabout is fair play."

"That's fine with me," Hill told her. "Catching's an easy job. Pitching, on the other hand, takes a lot of skill."

"Oh, so you think catching's easy," McBride growled. "Well, at least I can get it over the plate without pitching underhand."

"Now, boys, just hush up that bickering. Go on out there and do like I told you."

"There's only one thing, Ma," Mike said. "I don't think I can play without my shin guards and chest protector. I'm so used to wearing them. I'd like to keep my mask and catcher's mitt, too."

"And I'll catch with my pitcher's glove," Hoss told her.

"Any way you want to do it is all right, so long as you don't let those Bluejays score any more runs," Ma said.

"Cardinals, Ma."

"I knew they was some kind of birds. And one thing more. When Lefty Joe Rasmussen comes to bat, don't make him look bad. I know he's playing for the other team, but he's my hero."

McBride trotted out to the pitcher's mound in his catcher's garb. Hoss Hill crouched behind the plate.

110

The St. Louis players were laughing so hard at the spectacle of a catcher pretending he was a pitcher that none of them hit the ball out of the infield that inning. Big Noise Winnetka, who'd had trouble finding an aspirin, got back just in time to see the third out. He gave a yell of protest when he saw McBride pitching and started out on the field, but Ma Fuller grabbed onto his shirttail and pulled him back.

"Now don't go and spoil the boys' fun. Besides, take a look at the scoreboard."

There was no arguing with that nice round zero that had gone up for the St. Louis half of the inning. Later in the game, the Cards started to hit McBride's pitches fairly freely, but by that time the Gnats were five runs ahead.

In the last of the ninth, the Cardinals had crept up to only one run behind. The first man hit a fly to right and Fibich caught it. This so startled the next batter that he struck out. But then Lefty Joe Rasmussen came to bat and hit a clean single to center. Ma jumped up and down in front of the dugout, cheering him.

"How can you, Ma?" Johnny Hobbes asked. "That puts the tying run on base."

"Never you mind that. Lefty Joe wouldn't have liked it if he'd had to make the last out. Now we'll get this next batter and everything will be okay."

But the next batter didn't cooperate with this plan. He hit one to the right of Satchel-Foot Mooney, the nearly immobile second baseman, who tried desperately for it and missed it by several yards. That put runners on first and third. Winnetka started up the dugout steps. He had decided that the time had come to end this foolishness and put in a genuine pitcher. But Ma Fuller tugged at his shirttail.

"Now don't you go out there and hurt that nice Mr. McBride's feelings. He's doing the best he can."

"But one more hit and the Cards will tie the game."

"Never you mind. Mr. McBride is trying hard. Let him be."

Mike was trying hard. He was still wearing his catcher's paraphernalia, although it was getting uncomfortable. He had never realized before how much exercise a man could get pitching in the hot sun. He wiped his forehead and peered wearily down at Hoss Hill, who waggled his pitcher's glove at him.

McBride stretched his arms above his head, then threw the ball with all his might. The batter swung hard. To Mike's horror, he saw the ball coming like a bullet straight for his head. He started to move his catcher's mitt up to block it, but he knew in the instant of truth while the ball got larger and larger that the mitt would never get there in time.

The ball smashed into his mask. The metallic clang could be heard in the farthest reaches of the distant bleachers. McBride bounced back several feet. The ball shot high in the air. Hoss Hill was waiting for it when it came down. He threw it to first to get the runner by several feet.

"Now you see why I let Mr. McBride take over the pitching?" Ma asked Winnetka, triumphantly. "If we'd had some young fellow out there without that bird cage over his face, he might of got hurt."

☻ 12 ☻

Wɪᴛн a lifetime pitching record of one and nothing, Mike McBride decided to retire undefeated. It had been all right for a while, he told the manager, but catching line drives on his mask made his ears ring. The victory evened the series at one game apiece and put the Gnats five games out of first again. If they could win the third game with St. Louis, they could cut this margin to four.

And win it they did. It was not exactly a pitcher's battle—the Gnats didn't really have any pitchers of major-league caliber now that Five-Yard was playing center field. But it counts just as much in the standings to win a game fourteen to thirteen as one to nothing.

The Braves were next. The Gnats had to make the trip without Five-Yard. He was needed to play fullback for the Knights. Ma Fuller swooped down in her helicopter and picked him up, delivering him to the football field just before the game started.

"Now I know you've missed all our practice sessions, Five-Yard," Coach Murray Ding said. "But just play like you did last year and we won't have any problems. When they give you the ball—"

"I know. I carry it down between them posts there. Right?"

"Right. And if anybody gets in your way, knock him down."

"Okay. Of course, after I've scored, I'll come back and pick him up and maybe apologize."

The Knights won, with Five-Yard scoring three of their four touchdowns. As soon as the field was cleared, Ma came spiraling down in her helicopter. He hopped aboard, still wearing his helmet and football suit.

"How'd the Gnats do today, Ma?" he asked as they rose up over the stadium roof.

"We won, twenty to eighteen."

"Great. Who pitched?"

"Satchel-Foot Mooney. He said if a catcher could win a game, a second baseman ought to be able to do as well. Mr. Winnetka's thinking about starting Mr. Four-Fingers tomorrow."

"That makes sense. All you need to throw the ball is four fingers and a thumb, so he ought to do all right."

Big Noise decided against using Fibich on the mound, however. It wasn't so much that he was afraid he couldn't pitch. Almost anyone could pitch as well as the Gnats' regular pitching staff. But Mike McBride came to Winnetka before the game and declared that the plan just wouldn't work out.

"What's going to happen when I catch the ball and throw it back to Four-Fingers?"

"He'll miss it, naturally."

"Right. Now that won't matter when nobody's on base, except it'll make the game go pretty slow while he's fumbling around, trying to pick up the ball. But suppose the Braves get a man on. He'll be able to steal at least one base every time I toss the ball back to the pitcher's mound and Four-Fingers fumbles it."

So Fibich stayed in the outfield and Winnetka went back to using his regular pitchers for the Braves series. The Gnats were still in a hitting streak and scored enough runs to take three out of the four games. They might have won the other except that when Five-Yard fielded a grounder with two men on base he grabbed the ball and started to run with it instead of throwing it to the infield.

Everyone agreed it was a natural mistake for a fellow who was trying to play baseball and football almost simultaneously. Besides, there was no point in criticizing someone who had hit five home runs in the last three games and raised his season's batting average to .456.

While the Gnats were winning three of four, the Cards had lost four straight games in Los Angeles. To its surprise, Winnetka's team found itself only one game out of first place.

Hardly anyone had really believed the Gnats had a chance to win the pennant. The team's rise in the standings had been looked on as a freak development that would soon end and allow things to get back to normal. Now, with a week of the season left, fans around the country began to ask each other:

"Hey, is it possible that a team like the Gnats can become the league champions?"

And this was naturally followed by an even more puzzling question:

"If they do, can baseball survive?"

Among those who began to take the Gnats' chances seriously were the members of the New York Gnats. They began playing like men who had suddenly discovered they weren't in the game simply to give the sport some comic relief. The pitching staff started to bear down. It managed to hold the batters to an average of six runs a game in the Pittsburgh series. That was not very good by most standards, but it was better than the Gnats' pitchers usually did. The team took all three games from the Pirates. Meanwhile, the Cardinals felt the breath of their pursuers and won three straight from Houston, to keep a one-game lead. The Gnats split two games with the Cubs. St. Louis lost two games to Cincinnati, so when the Cardinals arrived for their final series with the Gnats the teams were tied for first place, with just three games to play.

"All we've got to do is take two out of the next three," Johnny Hobbes reminded the manager.

"We've got to win the ones today and tomorrow," Winnetka said. "Otherwise we're out of luck."

"You've given up hope of winning the final game?"

"Just about. It's on Sunday and Five-Yard will be playing football for the Knights that day over on the other side of town. I tried to talk Ding into letting us have him, but Murray says he's got a game of his own to worry about. Doesn't he realize that baseball's the national pastime?"

"Those football types never seem to understand that," Hobbes said. "Well, if we take the games today and tomorrow it won't matter whether Five-Yard's available Sunday."

The Gnats did win the first game, putting them in the lead in the pennant race. The St. Louis manager made the error of having his pitcher let Five-Yard hit instead of walking him and before he'd realized his mistake Five-Yard had driven in five runs during his first two times at bat. The final score was five to four.

In the dugout after the game, the team members started yelling and pounding each other on the back. But Big Noise put a stop to the celebration.

"Win one more, boys. Then you can whoop and holler all you want."

"We'll win it easy," Satchel-Foot Mooney shouted. "The Cards are choking up. When a team scores only four runs against one of our pitchers, it means the choke is on."

The next day's game was a different story, however. The Cardinals scored nine runs before anyone was out in the first inning and went on to win by a score of fourteen to three. The teams were tied again with just one game to go.

"I sure wish I was going to be able to play today," Five-Yard told Four-Fingers Fibich as they shared a table at breakfast the next morning.

"Me, too, Five-Yard. But we'll just have to do the best we can. There's no chance of you getting back in time for an inning or so?"

"I don't see how I can. The football game with the

Giants starts about the same time as the one with the Cards, and it's clear across town."

"Ma Fuller will be standing by with her helicopter."

"Even Ma can't put me in two places at the same time. You'll just have to win without me."

"We'll try," Fibich said, grimly. "We've come this close. I'd hate to see us blow the pennant now."

Winnetka tried to appear cheerful as the team took infield practice before the game, but he couldn't fool anyone. He certainly couldn't fool himself.

"It's a shame, Johnny," he told Hobbes. "All my life I've wanted to be the manager of a pennant winner. When I agreed to work for the Gnats, I thought I'd never have a chance to do it. And now I'm so close to it. But I'm afraid the boys can't do it without Five-Yard."

"They're going to do their best. I never saw them take anything so seriously. Do you know that Satchel-Foot Mooney came out here this morning and ran around the stadium twice, so he'd be loosened up."

"How long did it take him?"

"About an hour for each lap. I got here just as he came puffing into home. I asked him what he was doing and he said he'd decided to be ready in case we wanted him to steal second."

"I wondered why he was so tired out. He could barely walk to second base, let alone run. But I give him credit for trying, anyway."

The football game between the Knights and the Giants drew a capacity house even though the most important game of the baseball season was being played across town. When it began, Five-Yard lined up with the others, but his mind wasn't on football. He kept wondering how the Gnats were doing.

"I feel like I'm letting them down, being here when they need me there," he told Moose Walpurgis during a time out.

"Just remember we need you, too. This Giants team is plenty tough."

The Knights scored first. Five-Yard caught a pass just beyond the line of scrimmage. A wall of burly tacklers bore down on him and for a moment he regarded them with mild surprise. Then he remembered he was playing football instead of baseball and he went plowing through them, scattering them left and right, and kept on going across the goal line.

The Giants came back to tie the score on a long pass. Then, after the Knights' quarterback fumbled, the Giants pushed down the field to score again. At halftime, the Knights were still seven points behind.

"You happen to hear what the score was?" Five-Yard asked Moose as they went into the dressing room.

"Sure. The Giants are ahead, fourteen to seven."

"I don't mean that score. I mean the Gnats' game."

"Forget it," Coach Murray Ding ordered. "This is the game you're supposed to worry about. Now get out there next quarter and score some touchdowns. You've been playing as if your mind was on something else."

The Giants made another touchdown and a field goal in the third quarter. The Knights got one of the touchdowns back as the fourth quarter opened, putting them ten points behind, and scored another as the clock ticked toward the end of the game. With less than a minute to play, they got the ball back deep in their own territory. Murray Ding grabbed Five-Yard's shoulder.

"We're behind twenty-four to twenty-one. Now I'm depending on you to go in there and do something about it."

"You want me to score a touchdown?"

"I wouldn't mind. I wouldn't mind at all."

"What'd you say the score was, Mr. Ding?"

"The Giants are ahead by three points."

"Oh, I don't mean in this game. I was wondering what the score was in the Gnats' game with the Cards."

Ding threw his hat on the ground and jumped on it. Five-Yard decided that the coach was embarrassed because he didn't know the score of the other game. He trotted onto the field. The ball was snapped. Five-Yard grabbed it and started downfield. But three Giants tacklers bore him down.

"I only made about twenty yards," he told the quarterback, apologetically. "But try me again."

"They'll be expecting that. I think I'll try a pass."

He did try one. In fact, he tried two. Both fell short and that left eighteen seconds remaining with the Knights still three points behind.

"Okay, Five-Yard," the quarterback said, grimly. "It's up to you."

Fuller nodded. He lunged forward when the ball was handed to him, holding it high over his head so no one could grab it out of his hand. He shook off one tackler and kept going to midfield. Then four Giants' players converged on him. One grabbed his shoulders.

Another pulled at his legs. He felt himself going down.

Then he saw Ma Fuller's helicopter. It came soaring in over the stands behind the goal posts. He could see her waving to him to hurry up.

"Okay, Ma," he yelled. "Just wait right there."

With a heave of his shoulders and a thrust of his legs, he shook off the tacklers and took off toward the goal line, still clutching the ball. The Giants' safety man loomed ahead of him.

"Sorry," Five-Yard said as he pounded toward him. "I'm in kind of a hurry. Ma wants me."

The safety man found himself flying through the air to sprawl on the turf while Five-Yard went thundering across the goal line. The final gun sounded. The helicopter came swooping down. He jumped aboard as the figures went up on the scoreboard to show that the Knights had won.

"What's the score, Ma?" he demanded as the helicopter zoomed up over the stadium wall. "And don't tell me the Knights' score. I already know that."

"I been listening to the Gnats' game on the radio," Ma said, as she set a beeline course for the ball park. "The Cards scored three in the first half of the ninth, so now they're ahead six to four."

"Then we've still got a chance. Can you get me there before the game's over?"

"Hang on, son. We're about to set a new speed record for crosstown helicopter flying."

☙ **13** ☙

FOUR-FINGERS FIBICH was the lead-off batter in the last half of the ninth inning. Big Noise gave him his instructions.

"Get on base. We've got to tie the score this inning or we've lost the series."

"Don't you worry," Fibich told him. "All it takes to get a hit is four fingers and a thumb."

"It might be better if you used eight fingers and two thumbs," Winnetka advised him.

Fibich strode to the plate, swinging three bats. The umpire had to remind him to throw two of them away. Then he dug in his heels and swung at the first pitch.

"A triple!" Johnny Hobbes shouted. "That's got to be at least a triple."

It might have been, except that Fibich failed to take his turn at first base. For a moment, Big Noise wondered if Four-Fingers would keep on running all the way to the right-field wall. But he didn't. He skidded to a stop, ran back to first and started down toward second.

"Maybe a double," Johnny Hobbes said. "Even a double wouldn't be too bad."

The center fielder had the ball and was preparing to throw it. Fibich heard the crowd yelling. He turned to doff his batting helmet politely. This was a mistake. His feet got tangled up. He went sprawling. He managed to pick himself up and scramble back to first just ahead of the ball.

"A single," Hobbes said. "At least he's got a single. And there's nobody out."

"Come on, Mike," Winnetka urged. "Get hold of one."

McBride nodded resolutely. He pounded the dirt from his spikes. He scowled menacingly at the pitcher.

"Put one across," he growled. "I dare you."

The St. Louis pitcher did put the ball across the plate. In fact, he sent it across the plate three times, with Mike swinging and missing. Mule Bradshaw, who was up next, fouled off several pitches and finally drew a walk. That put runners on first and second. But then Skeeter Ferrara popped out to the second baseman and the Cardinals were one out away from the pennant.

Lefty Lecos was due to bat next. Lefty was having a better year than anyone had expected. He was batting .190. But Big Noise wondered if it wouldn't be a good idea to try a pinch hitter. He glanced down his bench. Then he shook his head. None of the available batters was hitting over .150.

Winnetka turned his eyes away from the collection of sure outs. He raised them toward heaven, not in the hope of finding help there but in a mute appeal. Then he jumped to his feet and pointed.

"She's coming. Stop the game. She's coming!"

For months, Dusty Hornbostel, the home-plate umpire, had been looking forward to the end of the season. Now that it was nearly over he was getting impatient. He wanted to put on a checked sports jacket and forget he'd had to spend all these hours standing in the hot sun wearing a blue coat whose pockets bulged with baseballs. He glanced angrily at the Gnats' bench.

"Let's go. Get a batter out here. Play ball."

Big Noise strolled out toward home plate. "But she's coming," he explained. "I can see her helicopter zooming along over the rooftops. Ma Fuller's on her way."

"I'm not interested in what's new in aviation," Hornbostel said. "I just want to get this game over so I can go out and have a good steak and forget I'm an umpire. It's a modest ambition, but my own. Now if you'll just get your next batter up here, we'll get this thing over with."

"My next batter's on his way, I tell you. I'm going to put in a pinch hitter."

Hornbostel put his hand above his eyes and peered around. "I don't see him."

"Of course you don't see him. He's up in the sky. He's zooming over the rooftops."

The umpire took off his mask. He put a fatherly hand on Winnetka's shoulder.

"I always figured it'd happen some day, Big Noise. I

always figured it was asking too much of a man to expect him to manage the New York Gnats for a living. Now why don't you just go over in the dugout and lie down?"

"I don't want to lie down. There's nothing wrong with me."

"Of course there isn't. You've just flipped your lid, that's all. It could happen to anybody. If I was the Gnats' manager, I'd probably see pinch hitters in the sky, too."

The fans in the bleachers had heard the helicopter by now. They peered up to see what was coming. Ma zipped over the wall, then hovered over the stands while Five-Yard leaned out and yelled down a question.

"How many outs?"

A small man with a mustache stopped chewing peanuts long enough to act as spokesman.

"Two out, two on," he shouted. "You going to bat?"

"If Mr. Big Noise wants me to."

"Oh, he'll want you to," the small man said. "Say, would you mind hitting the ball to me? I'd like to bring home a souvenir to prove to my wife I was at the ball park."

"I'll try," Five-Yard shouted down, clinging to the sides of the open window.

"Blanche won't give me such a hard time trying to prove where I've been if I bring her a baseball souvenir," the fan said. "So I'd take it as a special favor."

"Enough of this folderol," Ma Fuller said, slamming the canopy shut. "Hang on, son."

The helicopter came fluttering across the diamond like an awkward owl. It hovered above home plate.

126

Big Noise looked up at it joyfully. Dusty Hornbostel regarded it in deep disgust.

"Women drivers," he said. "I can't get away from 'em even in the ball park. Baseball wasn't like this back in the days when I was playing for the St. Louis Browns."

"There's my pinch hitter," Winnetka said, gesturing aloft. "Now if you'll just call time while Ma lands—"

"I'll do nothing of the sort. And neither will she. This is a no-parking zone. I've just declared this diamond off-limits to helicopters."

"But that's my best batter, hovering up there twenty feet in the air."

"I can't help it. If that machine touches so much as a blade of grass on this diamond, I'll declare the game forfeit and the Cards will be the champs." Hornbostel shook his fist at the helicopter. "Shoo. Get out of here."

"What's the matter, Mr. Big Noise?" Five-Yard asked, peering over the side of the machine.

"He says you can't land."

Five-Yard turned to Ma Fuller. "He's the umpire. We can't win an argument with an umpire. It looks like I'm not going to be able to bat after all."

"Nonsense, son. Look under the seat. I've got a present there for Pa."

"That's right nice of you, but how's that going to help?"

"It's a coil of rope, boy. I was planning to give it to him so's he could use it on his hay fork. I knew it was the kind of thing he'd like to have me bring him from the big city. But we can use it now. Just tie it to the seat there and toss it over the side."

Five-Yard did as he was told. Then he grasped the

rope and let himself down, hand over hand. Dusty Hornbostel watched him descending in mingled disgust and disbelief.

"There's got to be some kind of a rule about this," he said. "He's got to be violating some kind of a rule."

"You just show me in the rule book where it says how a pinch hitter is supposed to get to home plate," Winnetka shouted, waving his arms. "It doesn't say a word about it—whether he's supposed to run or walk or climb down a rope from a helicopter."

"Well, I know one thing," Hornbostel said. "The rule says a player's got to be in the proper uniform of his team. It doesn't say anything about him coming to bat wearing a football helmet and shoulder pads."

"That is the uniform of one of Five-Yard's teams. Of course, if you want to call time out and give us a couple of minutes, we can have him change."

"And make me postpone having my steak that much longer? Nothing doing."

"Then you've got to let him bat," Winnetka said, triumphantly. He turned to wave at Ma, who was still hovering overhead. "It's okay," he shouted above the noise of the whirling blades. "And thanks for getting him here on time."

"Nothing to it," Ma yelled down. "Now I'll just back this contraption off and set up there over the bleachers and watch my boy win this game. Or is there some fool rule about that, too?"

"I don't remember seeing one."

"That's surprising. You men and your games—always making rules to get things complicated. Well, here I go."

She revved up the engine and swooped out to hover above the flagpole.

"Play ball," Dusty Hornbostel said, wearily. "I can't stand much more of this."

The St. Louis manager had come toward the plate to argue about letting Five-Yard drop in so unexpectedly, but he saw the expression on the umpire's face and decided not to push him too far.

"I just want to say that I'm playing this game under protest," he announced.

"And I'm umpiring it under protest," Hornbostel growled. "Now go sit down. Let's get this over with. Play ball!"

Five-Yard glanced around the infield, noting the two runners on base. He looked at the scoreboard, showing the Gnats had two outs and were two runs behind. Then he stepped out of the batter's box and called time.

"Now what?" Hornbostel demanded.

"I can't find him. And a promise is a promise."

"I don't know what you're talking about." Dusty turned to Winnetka. "Get this man of yours back in the batter's box."

Five-Yard told the umpire he was almost ready to bat, but first he wanted an announcement made over the public address system. Winnetka listened to the request in astonishment, but he didn't argue. He hurried over and told the stadium announcer, who picked up his microphone and sent his voice booming out to the bleachers:

"Will the little man with a mustache whose wife, Blanche, wants a baseball please stand up and wave?"

Everyone looked around to see which fan the announcer meant. Five-Yard put his hand up to shade his eyes and peered out at the bleachers. He finally spotted the man frantically waving in the sixth row.

Five-Yard waved back, politely. Then he stepped into the box. The St. Louis pitcher, under orders not to give Fuller anything good to hit at, took a deep breath and let fly. The bat swung.

In the instant the bat met the ball, the resounding crack told everyone in the park that the season was over and the Gnats were champions of the league. Five-Yard trotted around the bases with the winning run while everyone in the stadium stood and cheered and threw their hats in the air and pounded each other on the back.

Everyone stood, that is, except a small man with a mustache, who sat in the sixth row of the bleachers, nursing a bruised right hand and admiring a battered baseball.

"Blanche will be so happy," he told the fellow next to him. But the stranger was so busy yelling and jumping up and down that he didn't pay a bit of attention.

⊝ 14 ⊝

THE New York Gnats were the champions of the National League. This was such an astounding development that the nation's baseball fans could hardly believe it. Mushmouth Flang, the world-renowned television announcer, had seen it happen. But he could hardly believe it, either.

"Statistically," he explained to Ted Hobbes after the broadcast was over, "it's impossible. It couldn't happen that players with the kind of past records that the Gnats have, could win the pennant."

"But they did, Mushmouth."

"Yes, thanks to that kid, Fuller. But wait until they meet the Yankees in the World Series. The Yanks'll slaughter them."

Even the gloriously happy Gnats' followers would have agreed with that prediction. While they celebrated their team's triumph, the fans felt little twinges of anxiety every time they thought of what would happen when the Gnats had to walk out on the same diamond with the mighty Yankees.

Most of the Yankee players, like the fans, assumed the Gnats would lose the Series in four straight games. But the Yankee management took nothing for granted. The manager, Aldous X. Sitwell III, held a strategy session with his coaches just as though he was going to have to play a real championship team instead of the Gnats.

"Now, gentlemen," Aldous began, for he was the leader of a very gentlemanly group, "I realize the Gnats don't belong on the same diamond with us. They're upstarts. They're uncouth. Aside from some clodbuster named Fuller, who appears to have some natural talent, they're a collection of misfits from the wrong side of town. Still, the Yankees did not become the most successful operation in the history of baseball by taking unnecessary chances. Even though we have to play only the Gnats in the World Series, we're going to use our first team."

"Do you really think that is quite necessary, sir?" asked the third-base coach, Clarence Wandheimer. "Some of the men had hoped to be able to leave early to take care of their far-flung business interests."

"I suppose the junior varsity could win handily enough," Aldous X. Sitwell III agreed. "Still, I am determined that those uncouth fellows from across town shall be taught a lesson for the good of baseball's image with the public. It is not enough simply to defeat them. We must smite them down, gentlemen. We must make the scores of our four victories so one-sided that the Gnats will slink away abashed. We must make sure that they become so discouraged that they will go back to their own league and return to their proper station in life next season."

"And that is, sir?"

"Their proper station in life, gentlemen, is tenth place."

Big Noise Winnetka held a strategy session, too. He called together his entire team. He climbed on a bench in the locker room to talk to them.

"I know what everybody's saying, boys. They're saying it was a fluke we won the pennant. They're saying we don't belong on the same field as the Yanks. Now, boys, what do you say to things like that?"

"We say they're all true, Big Noise," Fibich assured him.

"That's the wrong answer. But never mind. I didn't manage the worst team in baseball to a pennant without having a trick or two up my sleeve, I can tell you that. I've got a secret weapon for the Series that the Yankees can't match."

He jumped off the bench. He hurried over to the door. He opened it.

"Boys, meet the new assistant manager of the New York Gnats."

Ma Fuller was dressed in a baseball uniform several sizes too large for her. She had the cap cocked over one ear. The trousers drooped down over her shoe tops. The shirt billowed out like a sail. She made a comic sight, but none of the players laughed. Instead, as she came trotting into the room, beaming proudly

up at them, they cheered. Ma jumped onto the bench and raised her hand for silence.

"Never mind the whooping and hollering. We've got work to do. Now the first thing I want you boys to do to get ready for the Series is to straighten out your lockers. They're a mess."

"But, Ma," Hoss Hill protested. "What's that got to do with beating the Yanks?"

"A boy who doesn't pick up his socks doesn't deserve to win. And another thing I want you to do is go outside and help the ground crew tidy up the ball park. After all, we've got company coming. How would it look if the Yankees got here and the place wasn't neat?"

"Don't you think we ought to go out and practice playing ball?" Four Fingers inquired.

"Work first, play second. That's the rule for growing boys. Now everybody get busy with the chores and I'll go on back to the hotel and bake you all something special for dessert."

"Elderberry pie, Ma?" Hill asked, eagerly. "I just love your elderberry pie."

Something steely and grim came into Ma Fuller's blue eyes.

"You'll get your fill of elderberry pie as soon as you learn how to get the ball over the plate to those Yankee batters, boy, and not a minute before. But meanwhile, I'll whip you up a batch of loganberry upsidedown cake while you fellows are mowing the outfield and picking up the gum wrappers. Now skedaddle out of here and get busy."

The Gnats went reluctantly to their chores. Ma

headed back to the hotel, where she chased the chef out of the kitchen. Johnny Hobbes and Winnetka were left alone in the dugout.

"You think Ma knows what she's doing?" Hobbes asked. "I'll admit she's had some good ideas, like letting Mike McBride pitch with his catcher's mask on. But how is tidying up the park going to help beat the Yankees?"

"At least it'll keep the players' minds off baseball. The less they think about the Yanks, the better. Besides, watching Ma Fuller operate for the last few months, I've become convinced that she's a woman who can do anything she puts her mind to. If she decides our team is going to win the Series, the players won't dare lose."

The first two games were to be played at Yankee Stadium, which meant that the Gnats batted first. As Skeeter Ferrara led off, Ma Fuller took her place in the first-base coaching box. Over in the Yankee dugout, Aldous X. Sitwell III made a well-bred gesture of disgust.

"How utterly typical of those mountebanks from the wrong side of town to do a thing like this," he told Clarence Wandheimer. "A woman in uniform! We must teach them a lesson they shall not forget."

Ferrara and Mule Bradshaw struck out. Five-Yard was the next batter. He grabbed two bats and swung them around his head as he walked toward the plate. Ma called time out and motioned for him to come to her.

"I don't like to criticize, son, but the way I understand it you only need one bat at a time. I don't like to see you showing off by using two."

"Oh, I wasn't going to use both of them. One of these is what they call a practice bat. It's full of lead to make it heavy. You swing it around a few times and then when you throw it away the regular bat seems lighter and you can swing it harder."

"Sounds downright sneaky to me, boy. Now I tell you what you do. You just toss the regular bat away and use the one with all the weight in it."

"How come, Ma?"

"It'll make it fair. That pitcher the Yanks are using is such a puny fellow, a big boy like you ought to have some handicap. If you use the heavy bat, it'll kind of even things up."

"But this isn't the ordinary warmup bat the other fellows use, Ma. This is a special one Mr. Big Noise had made just for me. He said the regular one wasn't heavy enough to give me any exercise so he had a lot more weight added to this one. Nobody else on the team can even lift it, let alone swing it."

"Good. That'll be fair, then. Now you just go up there and take a good, healthy swing at the ball, son, like I'm telling you."

"But, Ma—"

"Don't you go arguing with me, boy. I'm your mother so I know best."

Speed Azalea, the Yankee pitcher, was said to have the fastest fast ball in the American League. He coiled himself into a knot when Five-Yard strode to the batter's box. Then he uncoiled and sent the ball hurtling toward the plate.

Five-Yard knew that with a bat that weighed over one hundred and fifty pounds he would have to use all his muscles. He had never tried using all his muscles at one time before because it had never been necessary. But now he did. He swung the heavy bat around his head a couple of times while Speed Azalea was winding up. Then as the ball came whistling toward the plate, he swung the bat again. It met the baseball squarely. The sound of the meeting could be heard as far away as Times Square, where it startled the pigeons.

Five-Yard headed toward first, but then he stopped, puzzled. The Yankee players stood around, looking at each other. Dusty Hornbostel, who had been given the honor of umpiring the first Series game behind the plate, stood leaning foward, his hands behind him, his mouth open. The Yankee catcher whirled on him.

"What happened, Dusty? What happened to the ball?"

"It broke into a million pieces," the umpire said. "It simply blew apart when Five-Yard hit it."

"So what's your ruling?"

"That's a good question. Let's see if I can figure out an answer. Some of the ball went foul, but most of it went fair, so it's a fair ball."

Five-Yard had stopped at first base. "Should I keep running, Mr. Dusty?" he asked. "It don't hardly seem right."

"It all depends on where the ball went," Hornbostel said. "Some of it no doubt went over the wall and some of it in the bleachers, so that would be a home run. But some of the dust is still sifting down in the infield, and you can't have an infield home run. Not while I'm umpiring."

"I could bat again," Five-Yard suggested.

"I'd rather you didn't," Hornbostel said. "I don't want to have to see a thing like that twice in the same inning. I knew I should never have taken up umpiring. First I have to rule on things like a pinch hitter who climbs down a rope from a helicopter. Now I have to rule on a baseball that disintegrates into dust. I wish I'd gone to school and learned an honest trade."

"You've got to make some kind of a ruling, Dusty," the catcher told him.

"Okay, then I will. My ruling is that Five-Yard gets credit for half a homer."

"You kidding? There isn't any such thing."

"Oh, no? Well, what else do you call it when part of the ball goes into the stands and part of it is still sifting down on the infield? It's half a homer and Fuller gets to take second base."

Both teams put up an argument. Winnetka came running out, waving his arms and complaining that as long as the Yankees didn't catch the ball his man had a right to run all the way around the bases. Aldous X. Sitwell III walked with dignity to the plate to point out that he felt it ought to be considered merely strike one. At the end of the discussion, Dusty Hornbostel repeated his ruling that Five-Yard had hit half a homer and was entitled to second base, and that was that. Four-Fingers Fibich came to bat next. He popped out to the second baseman and the inning was over.

Sidewinder Scroggs, the Gnats' starting pitcher, got

through the first two innings without allowing a run, although the Yankees had men on base almost constantly. In the third, with the game still scoreless, Five-Yard came to bat with Skeeter Ferrara on first base.

"I'd better use my old bat, Ma," Five-Yard suggested. "All it does when I hit the ball with this one is confuse Mr. Dusty Hornbostel."

But Ma shook her head. "Fair's fair," she said.

So Fuller obediently carried the one-hundred-fifty-pound bat to the plate. Speed Azalea turned pale. The Yankee infield moved back so far that the second baseman bumped into the center fielder and had to apologize. Five-Yard tried to ease up on his swing, but the bat was so heavy that it picked up a lot of momentum.

Once more the ball burst into a million tiny pieces. Having set a precedent, Hornbostel stuck with it. He ordered Five-Yard to take second base. That put Ferrara on third with one out. He scored on a long fly ball and the Gnats ended the inning with a one to nothing lead.

Before the Yankees went to bat in the last half of the third, Aldous X. Sitwell III called them to him.

"Gentlemen, it is not necessary to make speeches. You are the inheritors of a noble tradition. Yet, through some freak of fortune, you are losing a World Series game to a team that—except for one player, who shall be nameless—belongs in the Three-eye League. A team, moreover, that is led by a funny little woman in baggy pants. I ask you a simple question. What are you going to do to redeem yourselves?"

The Yankees talked it over among themselves and

decided the best thing to do to redeem themselves in the eyes of Aldous X. Sitwell III would be to go out and get a few hits. The Yankee batters began to send baseballs flying all around the outfield and by the time the Gnats came to bat in the fourth they were behind by nine runs.

At Big Noise's insistence, Five-Yard went back to using his regular bat the next two times he came up. Ma Fuller agreed after Winnetka told her it was wasteful to destroy brand-new baseballs the way her son had been doing. Five-Yard added two home runs to the two doubles Dusty Hornbostel had awarded him, but it didn't change the final result of the game, which was a one-sided Yankee victory.

The Yankees won the second game, too. The Series moved to Gnats Stadium with Fuller's team behind, two games to nothing. Winnetka decided he'd better have a talk with Ma.

"I appreciate your help," he told her. "But I guess I'd better take over the job of running the team again."

"Now don't you go getting in a tizzy. I've got a plan for today's game—the Fuller shift."

"The what?"

"The Fuller shift. I got the idea from watching football games on the TV down at the feed store. Just before the ball is snapped, did you ever notice how some of the football players run back and forth to confuse the other team?"

"I hate to bring this up, Ma, but this is baseball we're playing."

"Never you mind that. Now I've had the boys out practicing all morning and they're ready to go. Why don't you just take the afternoon off and watch a movie or something? That way, you won't get nervous."

It was a tempting suggestion. But Winnetka decided that, as manager, he had a duty to come to the ball park. Before the afternoon ended, he almost wished he'd stayed away.

⊝ 15 ⊝

Mushmouth Flang, the world-renowned television announcer, was the one who suffered most from the Fuller shift. He had to try to explain what was going on down on the diamond while the Gnats were in the field.

"And so here we are in the top of the first inning of the third game of the World Series," he began. "The sun is shining, the wind is from the west at seven-point-six knots and the Yankee leadoff batter is walking to the plate. His hat size is seven and one-half, his mother's maiden name was Edith Cassowary, his— But wait a minute, folks. Something unusual seems to be going on down there on the diamond. What would you say the Gnats' infield was doing, Ted, boy?"

"I'd say they were in a football huddle," Ted Hobbes said.

"That's exactly what it looks like, Ted, boy. Only

you and I know that this is the great American pastime, baseball. So obviously the players can't be standing in a circle near the pitcher's mound calling signals."

"But they are, Mushmouth. I can hear the signals away up here in the press box. I just heard Mule Bradshaw say, 'Eighty-four, twenty-seven, sixty-three, hike,' and then everybody started running to their positions."

"But they aren't going to their positions, Ted, boy. Sachel-Foot Mooney, the nearly immobile second baseman, is playing third. Chip Woods, the third baseman, is catching. Mule Bradshaw, the first baseman, is at shortstop. Mike McBride is on first instead of behind the plate and Skeeter Ferrara, the shortstop, is pitching. Is Ferrara listed as the pitcher of record?"

"No. According to my scorecard, Groucho McGarrity's the pitcher, Mushmouth."

"But he's playing second. Well, folks, I don't understand what's going on. But as I've told you almost anything can happen in this great game of baseball and we'll just have to do the best we can up here in the broadcasting booth to tell you what's going on. Skeeter Ferrara is taking his windup and— But wait a minute. He only looked like he was taking a windup. Instead, he handed off the ball to Chip Woods, who passed it to Satchel-Foot Mooney, who lateraled it to Groucho McGarrity, who threw the ball past the first Yankee batter for called strike one."

On the bench in the dugout, Ma Fuller dug her elbow into Big Noise Winnetka's ribs.

"That'll teach those big city boys not to look down

144

their noses at a team managed by Ma Fuller," she said. "Those Yankee batters are as confused as a flock of chickens in a hailstorm."

"I'm a little confused, too," the manager admitted. "Is the Fuller shift going to happen with every pitch?"

"Only every now and then. But the batters will be expecting it and worrying about it. They may be the champions of the American League, but they're only nine men. Any woman who puts her mind to it can confuse nine men without half trying."

The Yankees prided themselves on their professionalism. They took pride in never letting anything that happened on the field bother them. But having to bat without ever being sure of exactly who was pitching at any given moment confused them. All the scurrying about on the infield made the batters dizzy from watching it. With six different players taking turns pitching, depending on the signals called in the huddle held before each pitch, not a Yankee got a hit for the first eight innings.

The Gnats had their problems, too. Before long, the infielders were so tired from running back and forth that they could hardly lift their bats when it was their turn at the plate.

However, Four-Fingers Fibich was still full of energy. After deciding that the Fuller shift had so confused the opposition that he could take it easy in right field, he had been lying down there resting when the Yankees were at bat. So he was fresh as a daisy when he came to bat. Before the afternoon ended he got two doubles and a single. Sandy Dunes, the left fielder, had two singles. And Five-Yard came through as expected.

In the first inning he was held to a triple and in the third he grounded out. But in the sixth, he had the benefit of some advice from Ma Fuller and did better.

"The thing to do, son, is hit the ball over the wall. That way, it'll be hard for anybody to catch it."

Five-Yard did not believe in disobeying his mother. Two runners were on base when he hit the ball over the right-field wall, so that made the score three to nothing.

In the ninth, the Gnats almost threw the game away. It was Mule Bradshaw's turn to pitch, so he came running in from first to take the handoff from Mike McBride. The Yankee batter swung feebly and hit the ball back to the pitcher's mound. Mule grabbed it and started to throw to first, but no one was there. Groucho McGarrity, the pitcher, was supposed to be playing first, but he had missed the signal and was helping Satchel-Foot Mooney, the nearly immobile second baseman, play shortstop. That put a runner on first with the best Yankee batters coming up.

Seymour Scholl, the next Yankee batter, hit a tall fly ball out to right field. Four-Fingers Fabich had lost interest in the game and was lying on his stomach looking for four-leaf clovers in the outfield grass. Five-Yard yelled at him. He looked up just in time to see the ball coming at him. With great presence of mind he rolled out of the way and by the time he had scrambled to his feet and found the ball Scholl and the runner had both scored, cutting the Gnats' lead to three to two.

"This calls for a new pitcher," Ma Fuller said. She

looked down the bench. "Who hasn't had a chance to play today?"

"I haven't," Lefty Lecos said. "But of course I'm not a pitcher. I'm a center fielder."

"Then you're just the one I'm looking for. You go out and take Clarence's place in the outfield. Then when the signals are called, you come running in from center, grab the ball and fire a strike past the batter."

"That's a pretty long run, Ma. Do I have to?"

"You do if you want any dessert when I fix supper tonight."

Lefty didn't argue further. He took his place in the field. The Yankees, who had gradually become accustomed to being pitched to by whichever infielder happened to have the ball last, weren't expecting to have to deal with a center fielder, too. Before they had adjusted to this new development there were three outs and the game was over.

With the Yankees' lead in games cut to a two-to-one margin, things looked a little better for the Gnats. But on the day of the fourth game of the series, the Fuller shift had to be abandoned. The infielders were so lame and weary from their unaccustomed exercise of the day before that they simply weren't up to it. Ma said it was just as well.

"They'd be expecting the Fuller shift, so we'll try something different. Our strategy today, boys, is to go out and score fourteen or fifteen runs the first time we come to bat. Then we can relax a little."

But Aldous X. Sitwell III had decided on some strategy, too. Before the game, he had a talk with his pitcher, Red Scheller.

"I want you to give this Fuller person an intentional walk each time he comes to bat. Even if the bases are loaded, walk him."

"But is that quite cricket, sir? I mean, it's hardly befitting the Yankee image."

"True. That is why I've let the other men pitch to him during the first three games. But I have concluded that it would tarnish our public image more to get beaten by the Gnats than to walk their best batter intentionally. Don't you agree, old boy?"

"Definitely, now that you put it that way. Being defeated by the Gnats would be an unthinkable insult to our glorious tradition. I shall do as you suggest."

"Good show," Aldous said. "Now play ball, and may the better team emerge victorious."

After he had walked his first two times at bat, Five-Yard could see what was going on, but there didn't seem to be much he could do about it. Dusty Hornbostel said he wasn't allowed to leave the batter's box to reach for the ball and Scheller kept his pitches too far away for him to swing at them. After one of his walks he stole second base and scored on a hit by Chip Woods. But this was the only score the Gnats made. The Yankees won, five to one, giving them three games out of four. One more defeat and the Gnats would lose the Series.

Ma Fuller didn't like to play favorites. She considered all the team members her boys now. Still, she did have a special interest in her son, Five-Yard. She resented the way the Yankee pitcher had prevented him from hitting the ball.

"Fair's fair," she said. "A Fuller's got as many rights

149

as anybody else. Well, if that's the sneaky way those city boys are going to act, I'll just have to show 'em a thing or two."

When she posted the lineup for the fifth game, Hoss Hill hurried over to protest.

"You've made a mistake, Ma. You've got me down as the starting pitcher."

"Ain't you supposed to throw baseballs for a living?"

"Sure. But I'm not supposed to go in the game until after we're behind by ten or eleven runs."

"You were telling me just the other day that nobody gets many hits off you."

"And that's true. But that's because I usually throw the ball into the stands or some place."

"How do you know they could hit the ball if you threw it over the plate? You ever tried it?"

"Not during a game. I have good control while I'm warming up."

Ma said she couldn't understand why he could pitch strikes when there wasn't a batter, then lost his eye when the pitches counted for something. Hoss said it was easy to explain.

"I get nervous, Ma. All those people watching me and yelling and everything. Maybe if you'd keep them all out of the stands I could do better."

"Just don't pay them no nevermind, boy. Forget they're there."

"It's hard to forget about them when you've got fifty thousand people yelling at you. Besides, even if I could forget about the crowd, I'd still have to look at that Yankee batter standing up there at the plate. I get nervous just thinking about pitching against the Yankees."

"Well, you'll have to get over it, that's all. We've got to win this game to stay in the Series and you're the one who's going to do it. And if you do—"

She paused. Then she changed the subject, or seemed to.

"I got me a package in the parcel post from Pa Fuller this morning. He was rummaging around in the cellar and he found some stuff I canned while I was at home."

"Well, if you insist on me pitching, I'll do my best, but I don't think I—" Hoss suddenly thought of what Ma had been saying. A hungry glint came into his eye. "Say, that stuff Pa found—it wasn't elderberry pie filling, was it?"

"Nothing else but."

"And you wouldn't be planning to make some of my favorite pie for dessert, I suppose?"

"Well, now," Ma said, slyly. "It takes a little inspiration to make elderberry pie. A body has to be in just the right mood. If you was to go out there and beat those city fellows and show them who's boss, I wouldn't be surprised if that'd put me in just the right mood to make ten or twelve of the juiciest elderberry pies you ever saw."

"A dozen elderberry pies!" Hoss jumped to his feet and grabbed a baseball. "Get the oven hot, Ma. I'm going to get this game over fast."

One way to do it, he decided, was to throw nothing but strikes. After Mike McBride got over being astonished at his pitcher's newly acquired control, he suggested that Hill waste a pitch now and then by throwing it outside so the Yankee batters wouldn't expect everything to be in the strike zone. But Hoss shook his head.

"I'm getting hungrier with every inning that goes by," he said. "I want to get this game over. I want to hurry back to the hotel. And then I want to dive head-first into one of Ma's elderberry pies."

⚾ **16** ⚾

THE Gnats gave Hoss Hill a one to nothing lead in the fifth on an intentional walk to Five-Yard and a triple by Four-Fingers Fibich. This seemed like margin enough the way Hoss was going. Everything might have continued to be smooth sailing if Lefty Lecos hadn't mentioned the television cameras.

"Great game, Hoss," Lefty said as they sat on the bench and watched the Gnats going down in order in the bottom of the eighth. "One more inning and you'll have pitched a shutout. You'll be famous all over the country."

"Yeah, I suppose people will read about it in the papers."

"They won't have to read about it. They're watching it."

"You mean we're on television?"

"Naturally. And not just on the local station the way we usually are. We're on the network. Your picture is going into every home in the country."

153

Hill turned pale. "That's terrible. I forgot all about this being the World Series and how the game is going on the network. How many people you figure might be watching, Lefty?"

"Oh, maybe fifty million."

"Fifty million people! All of them looking at me. Oh, my."

Lecos saw he'd spoken out of turn. He tried to persuade Hoss that a lot of the television viewers might have turned off their sets during the commercials and forgotten to turn them back on, but the damage was done. Hoss could hardly walk to the mound for the top of the ninth, his knees were trembling so. He kept taking off his hat and smoothing back his hair and giving sickly little smiles in the direction of the cameras. Mike McBride hurried out to talk with him.

"Don't let up now, Hoss. You've got these Yanks eating out of your hand."

"I sure wish I'd got a haircut, Mike. Do you think people will notice on the TV that I'm getting a little shaggy around the ears?"

"Don't worry about that. Just get these next three batters."

"Do you suppose it'd be all right if I waved? I bet there's a lot of my old friends from my old home town watching. I don't want them to think I'm too stuck-up to wave."

McBride could see there was no use talking. He shook his head in disgust and trotted back behind the plate. He crouched down and signaled for a curve. Hoss nodded, wound up and threw the ball over Mike's head to the backstop. As the catcher accepted a new ball from the umpire, he noticed his pitcher grinning up toward the cameras and doffing his cap.

The first Yankee batter in the ninth walked on four straight wild pitches. The second batter walked, too. Then Hoss settled down a little on the third batter. He got the first pitch in the strike zone. The crowd, which had been getting restless, let out a cheer. Hoss's face turned red. He promptly walked the batter to fill the bases with no one out.

Over in the dugout, Big Noise jumped to his feet.

"I knew it was too good to last. Well, this has gone too far. I'm putting in another pitcher."

"Just simmer down now," Ma Fuller ordered. "I'm ready for this. I've just been waiting for the right time to use my secret weapon."

She reached into a paper bag she'd been holding on her lap. She pulled out a freshly baked elderberry pie. Then she trotted over behind home plate and held it up for Hoss to see.

"Strike out the side and you won't have to wait until you get back to the hotel," she told him. "Three more outs and it's all yours."

Mike McBride turned to protest. "Don't I get a piece?"

"Later. This one's Mr. Hoss's. Providing he does what I tell him."

Hoss did. Looking at the pie, he forgot the crowd. He forgot the cameras. He forgot the menacing Yankee hitter. He simply threw enough strikes to get the side out and the game over and then he headed straight for his reward. Ma handed it to him.

"Don't spoil your supper now."

155

"Oh, I won't. I'm just going to finish this off and then I'll go straight to the hotel and eat my meat and vegetables. On one condition, that is."

"What's that, son?"

"That I can have another of these elderberry pies for dessert. I seem to have worked up a pretty good appetite."

And so the Series stood at three games for the Yankees, two for the Gnats, as it moved back to Yankee Stadium. Ma Fuller, Big Noise and Johnny Hobbes held a strategy session on the morning of the sixth game, with Five-Yard invited to sit in as a representative of the players.

"I think we ought to move Five-Yard up in the batting order," Hobbes suggested. "Maybe let him lead off. As long as they're going to walk him every time, that'll give us a man on base and give the other guys a chance to knock him in."

"Good idea, even if I didn't think of it," Big Noise said. "Do you agree, Ma?"

"If the other fellows don't think he's getting pushy, batting first. I don't want anybody saying a Fuller's getting too pushy."

"Oh, they won't mind, Ma," Five-Yard said. "I just wish I could be more help to the team. Since my callus is gone, I can't pitch and now they won't let me hit the ball, either."

"They're scared of you," Winnetka said. "Not that I blame them. If I was Aldous X. Sitwell III, I'd do the same thing."

"Oh, I'm not blaming Mr. III," Five-Yard said. "He's just doing his job."

"Well, I blame him," Ma said. "Fair's fair and I

158

think every boy ought to have a chance to hit the ball and get some fun out of the game. But those city boys don't have no manners."

As usually happens in baseball strategy meetings, nothing much was decided except that it would be nice if the Gnats got a lot of hits and the Yankees didn't get many. Everyone agreed on this and the gathering broke up. Five-Yard went to his hotel room, which he shared with Fibich. Four-Fingers told him that he'd been lying there on the bed thinking about how to improve his fielding.

"You aren't doing so bad," Five-Yard told him. "Your fielding is better than it used to be. You're catching one out of every two or three balls that are hit to you."

"Yeah. Still, there's a little room for improvement. I've been thinking, as long as it's the World Series and everything, I might try catching the ball with both hands for a change."

Fibich got his chance in the Yankee half of the first. The first batter hit a hard line drive straight at him. Four-Fingers waited for it. He started to raise his gloved hand—the four fingers and thumb which, he had always contended, was all a man needed. But then he remembered his resolve to change his technique and he put up his bare hand, too. The ball passed between his outstretched hands and continued to the wall, with the batter getting all the way to third. He scored on a fly ball and the Yankees were ahead one to nothing.

The Gnats came back to tie the score in the fourth when Mike McBride singled, took second on a sacrifice by Sandy Dunes and came home on a hit by Satchel-

Foot Mooney. The Yankees scored three runs in the fifth and two in the sixth, but the Gnats made five runs on six straight hits in the top of the seventh so the game was tied once more. No one scored in the eighth, although the Yankees came close.

The first two Gnats made outs in the top of the ninth. But then Skeeter Ferrara beat out a bunt. Mule Bradshaw got an infield single. Lefty Lecos, batting for the pitcher, drew a walk. That brought up Five-Yard with the bases loaded.

Speed Azalea, the Yankee pitcher, called time out. He walked over to the sidelines to confer with Aldous X. Sitwell III.

"If I walk Fuller, I walk in the leading run, sir," he pointed out.

"And if you don't walk him, old boy?"

"He hits a homer."

"Then we have a choice of being one run behind or four runs behind, according to my mathematical analysis of the situation. Am I correct?"

"As always, sir."

"Then put him on. That means we'll be behind by a score of seven to six going into our half of the ninth, so it will be up to our men to score twice when we come to bat."

And so Fuller walked as usual, scoring Ferrara to put the Gnats one run ahead. The Yankee fans booed. The Gnats' fans yelled and stamped their feet. And Mushmouth Flang, the world-renowned television announcer, was the happiest man in the ballpark.

"We've just set a new record, folks," he told his listeners. "This is the first time in a World Series that a batter has ever been given an intentional walk with the bases loaded."

Fibich, who was up next, struck out. The Gnats took the field. They needed only three outs to tie the series at three games each. It looked for a time as though they would accomplish this easily enough. The first Yankee batter hit the ball hard but right at Satchel-Foot Mooney. If it had been a yard on either side he wouldn't have been able to reach it, but the nearly immobile second baseman was a good man with a glove if he didn't have to move his feet. So that was one out. The second came on a long fly ball to Sandy Dunes in left field.

"One more out, boys," Ma Fuller shouted. "Then we can go home to supper."

But the next Yankee batter walked. He took second on a wild pitch. Sidewinder Scroggs, the fourth pitcher the Gnats had used in the game, looked hopefully at Winnetka, who looked at Ma Fuller. But she shook her head.

"Let him pitch," she said. "He's no worse than the rest of 'em."

"And no better, either," Big Noise muttered.

He had a feeling of impending doom. A long single would tie the score. A homer would give the Yankees the game and the series. And the Yankees' best long-ball hitter, Zippo Wetzel, was coming to bat.

"Maybe we ought to walk him," Winnetka suggested. "First base is open."

"He doesn't scare me," Ma Fuller said. "Besides, if we walk him, that'll put the winning run on base."

There was logic in what she said, so Big Noise

nodded his head. But he still didn't like it. He didn't like the way Wetzel was scowling at the pitcher. When Zippo swung at the first pitch and missed it by a fraction of an inch, he didn't like the sound the bat made swooshing through the air.

Sidewinder didn't like the sound either. He sent the next pitch far outside, where Wetzel couldn't reach it. He wasted another pitch. But with the count two and one he had to get it in the strike zone. This time Wetzel connected.

Winnetka leaped to his feet. The ball was hit high and far toward right field. If it had been hit toward left or toward center, Big Noise would have felt a faint stirring of hope that someone would catch it. But Four-Fingers Fibich was the right fielder. That meant there was no chance at all.

Four-Fingers was ready to do his best, however. He ran forward a few steps. Then, realizing the ball would go over his head, he began to run backward as fast as he could go. He could hear the crowd yelling. He kept his eyes on the ball, which was getting closer and closer. As it approached, he gave a mighty leap.

He missed it by a good twenty feet. He fell sprawling. Frantically, he scrambled to his feet and turned to retrieve the ball, but it wasn't necessary. Five-Yard was there, holding it out to him.

"I hope you didn't mind my coming over here and catching it, Mr. Four-Fingers. I followed your advice. I grabbed it barehanded. Like you say, it only takes four fingers and a thumb."

"Oh, that's okay," Fibich told him. "I'm not mad at you for catching it. A young fellow like you, just learning the game, needs the experience anyway."

⊜ **17** ⊜

"**W**E just don't have a pitcher who's capable of starting this game," Big Noise Winnetka said.

"That's been true all season, except when Fuller was pitching," Johnny Hobbes said. "What's so different this time?"

"It's bad enough when the boys are fresh. But the pitching staff is so tired from the first six games of the series, they're even worse than usual. I've had to use so many relievers and keep so many people warming up in the bullpen that nobody's fresh enough to start."

"How about Hoss Hill?" Ma Fuller asked. "He did pretty well the other day."

"He ate so much elderberry pie after the game that he's out of condition," Winnetka said. "He might last for an inning or two, but not for a whole game."

"You've got eight pitchers," Ma said. "Let each of 'em pitch one inning. Fair's fair."

"How about Mike McBride?" Hobbes suggested.

"It won't work," the manager told him. "Dusty

163

Hornbostel says he won't stand for anyone being out of uniform. He'd never go for a pitcher who wears a catcher's mask and shin guards."

"I used to pitch a little myself when the boys was playing Three Ol' Cat," Ma Fuller said. "I never lost a game."

"I'll bet you didn't. But you're not on our playing roster. It's a shame you're ineligible. I'll bet you'd pitch a no-hitter."

"Well," Ma said, "if our pitchers can't hold those city boys our batters will just have to score more runs than they do, that's all."

Before the seventh and deciding game of the Series began, Ma Fuller made a little speech to the team. She told them that anyone who got a hit could have a second helping of dessert. But anyone who struck out would have to help wash the windows at the hotel.

"But, Ma, we're paying guests," Satchel-Foot Mooney protested. "We aren't supposed to have to work for our rooms."

"A little work never hurt anybody. Besides, any big strapping fellow who can't hit that puny little baseball with a big stick of wood ought to pay a penalty, that's what I say. Now get out there and score some runs so our pitchers won't have to take so many showers and use up all the hot water. After the game's over, I may decide to wash my hair."

The Gnats knew that Ma meant business. They took their turns at bat resolved to do as she asked. Skeeter Ferrara, who had gone back to the leadoff spot, got two strikes on him. But then he got to thinking about how many windows there are to wash in a twenty-two-story hotel and hit the ball into center field. Mule

Bradshaw hit a long fly ball that was caught. Five-Yard, who was up next, got his customary intentional walk.

"Gee, Ma, I wish they'd put the ball where I could smack it," he complained as he trotted down to first.

"Never you mind, boy," Mrs. Fuller told him from the first base coaching box. "Now just you pay attention to Mr. Four-Fingers up there at the plate. I've given him his orders."

"What'd you tell him to do?"

"Hit a home run."

"Oh, he'll try, I'm sure of that."

"I didn't tell him to try. I told him to hit one. And if he doesn't—"

Five-Yard never found out what might have happened to Fibich if he had dared to disobey Ma Fuller's instructions. Four-Fingers fouled off two pitches. Then, his expression grim and desperate, he took a mighty swing that sent the ball into the bleachers. That made the score three to nothing.

The lead didn't last, though. In the third inning, the Yankees knocked two Gnats' pitchers out of the box and scored five runs to put them ahead five to three.

The first man up in the fourth was Satchel-Foot Mooney, who got a long single to left. He didn't get a hit often, but when he did it was always a long one. It had to be. Unless the ball went nearly out of the park, Satchel-Foot could never beat the throw to first base.

Ma called time out so she could have a talk with Mooney.

"You did fine on that hit, boy. You made a single on what should've been a triple. You expect the Yankee pitcher'll be looking for you to steal second?"

"Hardly. He knows I'm the slowest runner in the history of organized baseball."

"What do you suppose he'd do if you tried it?"

"Well, first off he'd probably stand there on the mound having a real good laugh. Then he'd throw me out."

"The trouble with you is, your feet don't move fast enough." Ma glanced down. "And no wonder, with shoes as big as those. Take 'em off."

"But Ma, I have very tender feet."

"Never mind that. Take off your shoes and then when you steal second I'll give 'em back. It's no wonder you can't run, carrying those size-eighteen shoes around."

"But Ma, my feet are size eighteen, too."

Still, he did as he was told. Ma Fuller had one thing in common with an umpire. You couldn't win an argument with her. The Yankee players started pointing to Mooney's bare feet and making witty remarks. Ma told him to ignore them.

"They're city boys. They don't have no manners. Now do like I told you."

"This bare ground hurts, Ma."

"Cut out this nonsense and let's play ball," the first-base umpire ordered.

The Yankee pitcher took his stretch. He didn't bother to glance toward the runner. He knew that Mooney never even took a lead off base, let alone trying to steal.

"Skat!" Ma shouted as the ball left the pitcher's hand.

Satchel-Foot pounded toward second. He had told

166

her the truth about his feet. They were tender. Each time they touched the ground—and they touched a lot of it at a time—he could feel every imperfection in the infield. The solution seemed to be to touch the ground as seldom as possible. So he headed toward second in mighty leaps and bounds, like an overweight gazelle. It was not a beautiful example of running, but it covered a surprising amount of territory.

The Yankee catcher had the ball by now. He stood and watched the barefoot base runner in stunned astonishment. But then he snapped out of it and sent the ball speeding toward the second baseman. To his own amazement, Satchel-Foot arrived ahead of it, diving headfirst toward the bag. He explained later that he had decided it would be less painful to skid into second on his head than to travel any farther on his aching feet.

Ma gave him back his shoes. The Yankee pitcher was so unnerved by the experience of seeing Satchel-Foot leaping toward second that he walked the next two batters, filling the bases. Mule Bradshaw hit a long double that scored three runs and the Gnats were ahead six to five.

Hoss Hill was sent in to pitch and ordered to hold the lead. He was doing pretty well, too, until the Yanks got two men on with one out. The next batter bunted toward the mound. The ball stopped right at the pitcher's feet. Hoss started to bend over to pick it up and throw the runner out, but he found that he couldn't. After a season of Ma's cooking, topped off with all that elderberry pie, he simply couldn't bend far enough to reach the ball. So the bases were loaded.

167

Hoss lost his control at this point and walked in three runs before he was taken out of the game.

No more runs scored that inning, but the Gnats were behind eight to six. The Yankees added a run in the bottom of the seventh, making it nine to six, and almost scored again in the eighth. Ma Fuller and Big Noise used every pitcher in the bullpen to stop them.

"We've got nobody left to pitch," Winnetka said as the Gnats came to bat in the top of the ninth. "But I guess it doesn't matter. Unless we can make at least three runs and tie the score this inning, the game's over and the Yanks won't come to bat again anyway."

"That'll mean we've lost the Series," Ma said. "I never figured on that happening."

"It doesn't really surprise me. Anyway, we've done better than anybody expected. We've won three out of seven against a great team like the Yankees."

"We haven't lost this one yet. I told you I'd help you and the team become world champs, and a Fuller never goes back on her word. The Fuller honor is at stake. That's more important than a World Series. Who's up first?"

"I am," Satchel-Foot said. "But you'd better put in a pinch hitter. If you let me bat, I'm going to make sure I don't get on base."

"What do you mean by that?" Winnetka demanded.

"I'm not going to take any chances of winding up on first and having to take off my shoes again and steal second. I want to win this game as much as anybody, but it's asking too much of a man to expect him to go through torture like that twice in the same day."

"Oh, get on base," Ma said, impatiently. "I promise I won't make you steal. One run won't do us any good anyhow. We need at least four of them."

"Three of them to tie," Johnny Hobbes reminded her.

"It takes four of them to win," Ma said. "So we're going out there and get four."

Mooney walked to the plate. His feet still hurt, but he could swing a bat. He swung it and connected with the first pitch. The Yankee right fielder almost caught the ball but couldn't quite get to it and Satchel-Foot was on first.

Winnetka sent in a pinch runner. Chip Woods was up next.

"Don't you dare make an out," Ma Fuller told him. "Just get on base. I want three runners on when it's Clarence's turn to bat."

Woods didn't understand the strategy. Even if Fuller walked with the bases loaded, it would mean only one run. But he knew better than to argue. He stalked up to the plate and glared out at the pitcher.

"Your mother wears overalls," he shouted.

"What was that uncouth remark?" the Yankee pitcher inquired, unable to believe his ears.

"You heard me. And your grandmother—she wears overalls, too."

"My grandmother is a professor at Vassar," the pitcher declared angrily. "I'll teach you to make insulting remarks."

He took his stretch. He sent the ball heading high and inside to brush Chip back from the plate and teach him some manners. Woods saw it coming. He considered dodging out of the way. But then he remembered Ma Fuller's orders to get on base and he didn't move a muscle.

"You all right?" the umpire asked when they had picked Chip up off the ground.

"I'll live, I guess."

"That's a dangerous thing to do, standing there like that with a fast ball coming at you."

"Oh, no. The dangerous thing would be to make an out. Then I'd have to go back and explain things to Ma Fuller."

With two men on and no one out, Skeeter Ferrara popped out to the second baseman. Mule Bradshaw fouled off several pitches. Then he sent a vicious ground ball toward the shortstop. The infielder blocked the ball with his chest, but by the time he'd picked it up it was too late to make a play and the bases were loaded. The Yankee pitcher watched Five-Yard stride up to the plate. Then he called time and walked over to talk things over with his manager.

"An intentional walk as usual, sir?"

"Absolutely. That will score a run, but they will still be two behind."

"Good thinking, sir. When I get past this Fuller person I should have no trouble with the others."

Five-Yard had been talking with Ma while he waited. Now he stood in the right-hand batter's box as usual, his bat held loosely. The first pitch was carefully aimed several feet beyond his reach on the first-base side of the plate.

"Ball one," the umpire said.

The pitcher took his windup and sent the ball to the same spot. Five-Yard didn't move a muscle.

"Ball two."

Once more the routine was repeated.

"Ball three."

The catcher threw the ball back. The pitcher caught it and glanced around at the three base runners. Then he turned and threw what was to be the fourth ball.

But Five-Yard had stepped across the plate to stand in the batter's box on the first-base side. He had his bat on his shoulder, as though to bat left-handed. The catcher saw what was happening. He shouted a warning, but the pitcher had already let go of the ball.

Five-Yard turned, keeping his feet squarely in the batter's box, and waited for it. Then he swung his bat. The ball went on a rising line over the infield, over the outfield, and was still rising like a rocket as it cleared the left field wall.

Five-Yard trotted around the bases behind the jubilant runners. Every fan was on his feet, cheering. On the Yankee bench, Aldous X. Sitwell III sat with his head in his hands. For the first time since the Series began, he could believe that the impossible could happen. The Yankees could lose.

"But not to the Gnats," he told himself. "Defeat would not be so bad. But defeat by a team like the Gnats. . ."

The thought was too much to bear. He jumped to his feet. He stalked out to the mound.

"Get the side out. Get it out at once. Or else—"

"Or else?" the pitcher repeated, his face ashen.

"Or else I shall personally see to it that your face will never appear on another bubble-gum card."

⊗ 18 ⊗

THE Gnats scored no more runs, which meant that they took the field in the bottom of the ninth with the Yankees trailing, ten to nine. That is, eight players took the field. Neither Big Noise nor Ma Fuller could think of anyone on the roster who was capable of taking the pitcher's mound.

"My bullpen's empty," Winnetka said. "What am I going to do?"

"Hoss is all sweet and clean after his shower," Ma pointed out. "Why not put him in again?"

"Once you've taken a player out of the lineup, he can't go back in. The rules forbid it."

"Oh, you men and your rules. Always making things difficult."

Five-Yard, who had gone out to play center field, came trotting in to see what was holding up the game. Big Noise told him.

"Lecos can play center," Five-Yard said. "I'll pitch."

Hope stirred in Big Noise's heart. He grabbed Fuller's hand.

"The plowboy's callus has come back?"

"Nope."

"Then how can you pitch? You can't throw your garter-snake outshoot or yoyo. You can't throw your dogleg curve."

"I've still got my fast ball."

"Oh, no," Mike McBride said. He had walked over to get in on the discussion. "I'm not standing up there while you're throwing a ball that travels so fast I can't see it."

"The ump can't see it either," Winnetka pointed out. "We'll have to try something else."

"We haven't got anything else left to try," Five-Yard said. "Give me the ball. I'll figure out some way to win this game."

Winnetka turned to McBride. "Are you willing to take your chances?"

"All right. A man can't live forever, I guess."

There was a stir of excitement when Fuller walked to the pitcher's mound. Everyone in the stadium knew about his fast ball. The Yankees clustered around their manager, like chicks running to the mother hen when a thunderstorm approaches. They protested that it wasn't right to expect them to bat against a pitch they couldn't see.

"It doesn't frighten me a bit," Aldous X. Sitwell III assured them.

"I wouldn't be scared either if I was sitting on the bench," Larry Faulkner said. "But I'm leading off."

"From all I've heard about this Fuller person, he has perfect control. He'll throw nothing but strikes—only the umpire won't be able to see them, so he can't call them. Just go out there and let him walk in the winning run."

Faulkner moved reluctantly to the plate. Dusty Hornbostel turned to the catcher.

"All I've wanted is for the season to end so I could get out of this bulgy blue suit and into a smart sports jacket, Mike. Now I have to deal with something like this."

"I don't like it either," McBride told him.

"Neither do I," Faulkner said. "Why don't the three of us quit baseball and open up a nice quiet bowling alley somewhere?"

"Are you fellows ready?" Five-Yard asked. "I'm in no special hurry, but I'd just as soon go ahead and pitch."

"I don't suppose we'll ever be ready," Hornbostel said. "But let's get it over with. Play ball."

Five-Yard nodded. Mike McBride crouched down behind home, thrust out his glove and crossed his fingers. Faulkner waved his bat half-heartedly. The umpire leaned over to get as much of himself behind the catcher as possible.

Fuller coiled himself into a windup, then let fly. McBride looked down to find the ball in the pocket of his mitt. It surprised him, but he recovered quickly and glanced up at the umpire.

"Ball one," Hornbostel said.

"It was right over the plate."

"How do you know? You didn't see it either."

"I caught it, didn't I."

175

"Only because he threw it right into the pocket."

"That's where I was aiming," Five-Yard said.

McBride looked the umpire squarely in the eye.

"Dusty, I'm not trying to be sarcastic. I sympathize with your problem. I know you're an honest man. But can you really be sure that last pitch was a ball instead of a strike?"

Hornbostel started to bluster and get red in the face. But then he let his arms fall to his sides.

"I didn't see it," he said. "No one can see a ball that's going that fast. Time out. I want to think."

Hornbostel spent a lot of time complaining about his job, but deep down inside him he was proud of being an umpire. He took pride in his uniform, even if the pockets did bulge and spoil his profile. He took special pride in "calling 'em as I see 'em." But how could he call them when he couldn't even see a blur? It was a problem that he had never before faced in twenty years of umpiring. For the first time in a long career of split-second decisions, he couldn't decide what to do.

He walked over toward the home team's dugout and gestured for the rival managers to approach. Five-Yard came along, too.

"Gentlemen, I want to be fair to both sides," Hornbostel said. "This is the deciding game of the World Series. What we do here this afternoon will go down in the history of the game. I never thought I'd say this in public especially to a manager, but I'm in need of some advice."

"You can't see the pitches, old chap?" Aldous X. Sitwell III inquired politely.

"No one can see this kid's fast ball. There's nothing wrong with my eyesight, but I'm only human."

"Assuming for the sake of argument that an umpire is human," Aldous said, "it seems to me there is only one ruling you can make. If you don't see the ball go over home plate between the batter's knees and his shoulders, then you obviously must call a ball."

"Now just wait a minute here," Winnetka shouted. "If he can't see the ball go outside the strike zone, then it has got to be inside the strike zone. So he's got to call it a strike."

"What an uncouth line of argument," Sitwell said, sniffing. "The kind of uncouth suggestion I would expect from the manager of a team from the wrong side of town."

"I'm just as couth as you are," Big Noise shouted, shoving his chin against the other manager's jaw. "And quit shoving."

"Break it up or I'll throw both of you out of the game," Hornbostel yelled. "I've got troubles enough without you guys starting a rhubarb." He turned to Five-Yard. "Kid, it's your pitch that's causing all the trouble. You got any suggestion?"

"Gee, I don't know, Mr. Dusty. What does the rule book say?"

"It doesn't say anything about a fast ball that's invisible. You couldn't sort of slow down your pitches so I could see them, could you?"

"I'd sure like to oblige, but I can't. It's the only way I know how to pitch, now I've lost my callus. I learned back of the schoolhouse in Rock Creek. Playing against those guys—Crazy-Legs Walfoort and the rest

—if you didn't learn how to rear back and throw hard, they'd knock you out of the box."

"I'm surprised the other boys would play against you when they couldn't see the ball."

"Oh, Crazy-Legs Walfoort could see it all right. He'd kind of squint his eyes and crouch down and—"

"I know it's impolite to interrupt this fascinating discussion of life among your distinguished friends," Aldous X. Sitwell III said. "But we do have a World Series game to play, if you don't mind. If you can't decide this question, Hornbostel, why don't you call in an outside expert? The president of one of the leagues, perhaps, or the baseball commissioner."

"That's a pretty good idea, Mr. III" Five-Yard said. "But if you're going to get an expert, why not go right to the top?"

"The Chief Justice of the Supreme Court, maybe?" Hornbostel asked, sarcastically.

"He's probably pretty busy. I don't like to be the one to mention it, on account of it sounds like I was bragging. But we've got the biggest authority in the country right here on the field."

"The biggest authority on baseball?" Dusty asked.

"On baseball or anything else. Why, I remember the time she broke up an argument down at the feed store by explaining the best time to plant sweet corn is when the red oak leaves get as big as a gray squirrel's ear. And those experts down at the feed store don't give up easy."

"You mean Ma Fuller?" Big Noise asked. "You think she can figure out Dusty's problem?"

"Ma can figure out anything."

178

"But she's your mother," the Yankee manager pointed out. "She'd be prejudiced."

"Not Ma. Fair's fair, she always says."

"I've got nothing to lose at this point," Hornbostel said. "Call her over. Not that it'll do any good."

Winnetka waved. Ma Fuller came trotting over from the dugout, where she had been keeping the players busy picking up old bubble-gum wrappers. Hornbostel explained his dilemma. Ma nodded to show she understood.

"It appears like my boy, Clarence, ought to back up a mite, just to make it fair," she said. "If he was farther back maybe you'd be able to see the ball, Mr. Cornbustle."

"It's Hornbostel, madame. Maybe that'd help at that. Why don't we try it?"

"I'm willing," Five-Yard said.

"Well, I'm not," said Aldous X. Sitwell III. "The rules clearly specify that the pitcher must stand on the pitcher's mound."

"Oh, you men and your rules," Ma Fuller said. "Always making things more complicated for yourselves. I say change the rules a little and let's get on with this game without any more shilly-shallying."

"And I agree," Dusty said. "Maybe it's against the rules to pitch from behind the mound, but it's also against the rules for a ball to travel so fast an umpire can't see it. Or it ought to be."

The argument continued for a while, but Hornbostel stood firm. Finally, the Yankee manager agreed to try Ma's suggestion.

"Only my batter's got to be able to see the ball

179

plainly. And if he can't, Fuller's got to back up some more."

"Fair enough," the umpire told Sitwell. "Now let's play ball."

McBride crouched behind the plate again. The Yankee batter, Faulkner, nervously took his place. Five-Yard walked to a point halfway between the pitcher's mound and second base. He wound up and threw. The ball appeared in McBride's mitt.

"Anybody see it?" Hornbostel asked.

"Not me," Faulkner told him.

"I caught it, didn't I?" McBride demanded.

"Yes, but did you see it?"

"No. I sure felt it, though. I thought it was going to go right through my hand."

Hornbostel motioned to Five-Yard to back up farther. Fuller walked on back to second base. He asked Satchel-Foot Mooney, the nearly immobile second baseman, to move aside a little.

"But I always play with one foot on the bag," Mooney said. "That way I know where it is."

"I'm sorry, Mr. Satchel-Foot. But the umpire wants me to pitch from here."

"Well, okay. But don't blame me if I can't find the base again when it's time to make a putout."

This time when Five-Yard threw the ball, McBride claimed he caught a glimpse of it as it was heading toward his glove.

"I saw something, too," Hornbostel said. "But I think it was smoke, the ball was going so fast. He's got to back up some more."

It was not until Five-Yard was in deep center field

that the umpire was satisfied. He told him he could pitch from there. Lefty Lecos, for one, was pleased by the decision.

"It's lonesome out here in center field. It's nice to have somebody to talk to. You don't mind if I look over your shoulder while you pitch, do you?"

"Not a bit. And don't think I'm trying to horn in on your center fielding. If a ball comes out here, you can catch it."

"Okay. And if it gets over in right field, you take it."

"But Mr. Four-Fingers is playing there."

"I know. That's why I made the suggestion."

Five-Yard peered in at home plate. It was a long distance away. He saw McBride wiggling his fingers, but he couldn't make out the signal. But then, he'd never understood the catcher's signals even when he could see them. He cupped his hands over his mouth.

"You ready in there?" he shouted.

"Play ball," Dusty Hornbostel bellowed.

Five-Yard coiled himself into a knot. Then he uncoiled and the ball headed for the distant target of Mike McBride's mitt. It had slowed down enough by the time it crossed the infield so the batter caught a glimpse of it. But he was too shaken by all that had happened to swing.

"Strike one," the umpire said.

McBride started to throw the ball back to his pitcher. Then he realized it was too far. He threw it instead to Satchel-Foot, who relayed it to center field.

Five-Yard wound up again. This time, Faulkner took a mighty swing at the ball. He missed and it was strike two. Aldous X. Sitwell III called time. He walked out to talk to the batter.

"All you need to do is bunt it across the pitcher's mound," he said. "There's nobody there to cover."

"But it's the third strike. What if it goes foul?"

"Just see that it doesn't. We've got to get at least one run."

Faulkner nodded grimly. He waited until Five-Yard released the next pitch. Then he slid his hands forward on the bat and leaned over the plate.

It was a perfect bunt, except for one thing. Instead of bouncing feebly into the infield and rolling dead the ball was traveling so fast when it hit the bat that it went into the stands just to the left of the foul line.

"Foul ball," Hornbostel ruled. "You're out for bunting foul on a third strike."

But Faulkner was still standing there, his bat in his hands, his mouth open in amazement.

"Did you see where that bunt went?" he demanded. "If anybody ever gets hold of one of those fast balls with a full swing, it'll go clear to Albany."

Lecos decided he'd better play center field from the pitcher's mound, as long as the pitcher had taken over his regular place in center. In this way, the Yankees wouldn't be able to drop a bunt there without getting thrown out. But then a thought occurred to him.

"What if I'm standing on the pitcher's mound and one of your bullet balls hits me in the back of the head?" he asked Five-Yard.

"I guess it'd sting a little."

"I wouldn't feel a thing. My head would wind up in the press box. I'll tell you what. I'll lay flat on the ground in front of the pitcher's mound. Then after the ball passes me, I'll jump up and cover that part of the infield."

Five-Yard advised him not to jump up too soon. Lefty assured him he'd be careful. Still, seeing Lecos sprawled on the infield in a direct line between him and the catcher made Fuller cautious. He was so careful to throw the ball to one side to make sure Lecos would be safe if he popped his head up too soon that he walked the next two batters, putting the potential tying run on second and the winning run on first with only one out.

"One solid hit and we've lost the ball game," Winnetka told Lecos. "Get out of there. You're just in the way."

Lefty trotted back to center field. He told Five-Yard he was sorry.

"But all you've got to do is strike out the next two men and we're the world champs," he added. "How's your arm holding out?"

"It's getting a little tired. That's a pretty long throw to make on a straight line."

"All you need is six more pitches. Providing they're all strikes, that is."

Five-Yard could feel his shoulder muscles tightening. Six more throws would be about as many as he could make, he decided. He wound up and let fly. Dusty Hornbostel's hand went up. His voice came drifting out to center field.

"Strike one."

The next two pitches were also strikes and there were two away. But McBride noticed that the fast ball was beginning to slow down.

"I could see the ball coming when it got as far as

second base on that last one," he told Hornbostel. "How about letting Five-Yard move in a little closer on this batter?"

"Nothing doing. I've bent enough rules now without making any more changes. Play ball."

"Just three more pitches, Five-Yard," Lecos said, peering over the pitcher's shoulder from his station in center field. "Just three more strikes and the game's over."

"I guess I can manage three more throws," Five-Yard told him. "But that's plenty. My arm feels like I've been pitching hay onto a high wagon since sunup."

He looked at the runners. They were taking leads off first and second and he thought they might try to steal. But they were taking no chances on Five-Yard's arm. He took careful aim at McBride's distant mitt and threw.

The ball had slowed down appreciably by now, but it was still traveling fast enough so that the batter, Tin-Ears Armstrong, misjudged it. His bat barely touched it. The ball flew on a high arc over the roof of the stadium behind home plate.

"Foul ball. Strike one," Hornbostel roared.

Five-Yard put all his remaining strength into the next pitch. It went zipping across the plate so fast that Tin-Ears hardly saw it pass. And so the Gnats were one strike away from the championship. Over on the bench, Winnetka closed his eyes.

"I know something terrible's going to happen. It's got to."

"Why do you say that?" Johnny Hobbes demanded.

"Because if the Gnats win the world championship,

after all the insults I've had to take about being the manager of a rinky-dink ball team, it would be just too wonderful to be true."

"Don't worry, Big Noise. All we need is one more strike."

"And all they need is a long single to score two runs and win the Series."

Five-Yard caught the relay from Mooney. He stood looking at home plate, his powerful shoulders sagging. He had never felt this tired before. Pitching from center field was harder than he'd expected it to be. Still, he couldn't quit now, even if his right arm felt like it might fall off.

"One more, Five-Yard," Lefty Lecos said. "Then we can celebrate."

"One more pitch is one too many," Fuller told him. "I'm sure glad one is all it'll take."

He took a long breath. Then he brought his arm up and whipped it down with all his might, aiming for the corner of the plate.

Dusty Hornbostel hesitated. Then he made up his mind.

"Ball one," he said.

Mike McBride pulled off his mask and whirled toward the umpire.

"That was the prettiest strike across the inside corner I've ever seen," he shouted.

"I say it's a ball. And if you want to argue about it, you're going to get put out of the game. I've stood about all the nonsense I'm going to for one afternoon."

McBride muttered angrily to himself, but he put his

mask back on and threw the ball to second, where Mooney relayed it to Five-Yard.

"That's a shame," Lefty Lecos said. "It sure looked like a strike from here."

"If Mr. Dusty Hornbostel says it was a ball, I guess that's what it was. But I sure wish I didn't have to throw again. I'll be lucky if I can get it that far, let alone strike him out."

"Even if he hits it, remember we've got eight other players on the field." Lefty glanced toward right, where Four-Fingers Fibich was slapping his hand into his glove. "Or seven, anyway."

Five-Yard didn't bother to take a stretch. He didn't want to use up an extra ounce of energy. He simply drew back his arm and sent the ball toward home plate.

Tin-Ears Armstrong watched it approach in pleased amazement. It was going to be shoulder-high, just where he liked it. And by the time it reached him, he could see, it would be moving slowly enough so he ought to be able to knock it out of the park. While he was waiting, he began to make plans for spending the winner's share of the World Series check.

But despite his confidence, Tin-Ears miscalculated. He hit under the ball instead of meeting it squarely. Instead of smashing it out of the park he hit a towering fly ball toward right field. He threw down his bat in disgust. He began to trot toward first base, taking his time. But then a happy thought occurred to him and he picked up speed.

"Right field," he reminded himself. "Why, it couldn't

be better. Four-Fingers is in right. The game's as good as won."

Five-Yard had taken off toward right field the moment the ball met the bat. It was such a high fly that he might have a chance at it, he decided. As he ran, his long legs covering the ground in great leaps, he glanced up at the ball. It was going to come down just in front of Fibich. By dashing in ahead of him, he could grab it and the game would be over.

He had helped Four-Fingers cover right field once before, but then the ball had gone over the fielder's head and he had simply run behind him and caught it, backing him up. It would be humiliating for Fibich to have him snatch the ball almost out of his hands. It would be hard for him to stand around next season giving everybody free advice on fielding technique if the final out of the World Series was caught in deep right field by the pitcher.

As he ran, Five-Yard glanced at Fibich, who was circling around nervously under the ball, trying to decide where it was going to come down.

"If I let him try for it," Five-Yard told himself, "he'll miss it. We'll lose the game. But if I don't let him try—"

Suddenly, he stopped short, a few feet away from where the ball was rapidly approaching.

"Take it, Mr. Four-Fingers," he shouted. "It's all yours."

Fibich had been so intent on the ball that he hadn't heard Five-Yard approach. Startled, he took several rapid steps forward. He tripped. As he started to go down, he threw up his arms.

189

The ball arrived at the same moment. With a sigh of deep relief, Five-Yard saw it catch in the webbing of Four-Fingers' glove just before the right fielder fell to the turf and did a somersault in the grass.

In the dressing room, after the noise of the Gnats' celebration had died down, after everyone had pounded everyone else on the back and congratulated Five-Yard and themselves, the crowd began to thin out a little. Big Noise threw one arm around Fuller's shoulders and the other around Fibich.

"What a game," he shouted. "What a pitcher. And what a catch that was. I've said a lot of nasty things about your fielding, Fibich, but that diving catch makes up for everything."

The outfielder hung his head in embarrassment.

"Well, I didn't exactly—" he began.

But Winnetka wasn't listening. He spotted Ma Fuller beaming at her boys from across the room. He rushed over and lifted her up and whirled her around.

"Come on, Ma. One last meal to celebrate. I'm going to have seconds and maybe even thirds on your choke-cherry upsidedown cake tonight."

"Not until you boys clean up the mess you've made," she said, sternly. "The idea of throwing things around just because you've won a game. You'd think it was something important, like buying a new mule."

Five-Yard and Fibich were left alone in their corner. The outfielder turned to Fuller. He put out his hand.

"I been thinking about what you did, letting me take that fly when you could've caught it yourself and made sure of it," he said. "It was taking a big chance, but I sure appreciate it."

Five-Yard grinned. He took the outstretched hand and shook it.

"Why, I was hardly worried a bit. I figured the game depended on it, so you'd grab it. Besides, like you're always saying, there's nothing hard about catching a fly ball."

Fibich grinned back, full of confidence again.

"Right," he said. "Just remember what I've always told you. All it takes is four fingers and a thumb."

The Author

ROBERT WELLS wrote his first juvenile novel (*Five-Yard Fuller*) after a successful career as an adult writer of fiction and non-fiction for national magazines. It was inevitable that his tremendously popular story of the infallible bumpkin would create demand for a sequel, hence *Five-Yard Fuller of the N.Y. Gnats*. Bob Wells and his wife and family live in Delafield, Wisconsin.